W9-ADS-795

DISCARD

Farmer Boy
Goes West

LITTLE HOUSE · BIG ADVENTURE

Farmer Boy Goes West

HEATHER WILLIAMS

HARPER
An Imprint of HarperCollins*Publishers*

FOR JONAH
AND FOR DAD, MY OWN
HONEST-TO-GOODNESS HERO

Farmer Boy Goes West
Copyright © 2012 by HarperCollins Publishers
All rights reserved. Printed in the United States of America.
No part of this book may be used or reproduced in any
manner whatsoever without written permission except in
the case of brief quotations embodied in critical articles and
reviews. For information address HarperCollins Children's
Books, a division of HarperCollins Publishers, 10 East 53rd
Street, New York, NY 10022.
www.harpercollinschildrens.com

Library of Congress Cataloging-in-Publication Data
Williams, Heather.
   Farmer boy goes west / Heather Williams. — 1st ed.
      p. cm.
   Summary: After moving from Malone, New York, to Spring Valley,
Minnesota, in the 1870s, fourteen-year-old Almanzo Wilder, who
would grow up to become the husband of Laura Ingalls Wilder, and
his family must decide whether to stay out west or return home to the
life they have always known.
   ISBN 978-0-06-124251-9
   1. Wilder, Almanzo—Juvenile fiction. [1. Wilder, Almanzo—
Fiction. 2. Farm life—Minnesota—Fiction. 3. Family life—
Minnesota—Fiction. 4. Minnesota—History—19th century—Fiction.
5. Wilder, Laura Ingalls, 1867–1957—Family—Fiction.] I. Title.
PZ7.W662Far 2012   2011022937
[Fic]—dc23   CIP
                                                   AC

Typography by Michelle Taormina
12 13 14 15 16   LP/RRDH   10 9 8 7 6 5 4 3 2 1
❖
First Edition

CONTENTS

THE LETTER

A warm golden smell was coming from the kitchen window as Almanzo Wilder followed his father up to the house from the barn. The sky was gray, with a brisk wind pushing the clouds along and whirling fallen leaves across the path. The days were getting shorter, and autumn had come to upstate New York.

Almanzo liked the feel of the air in the fall. He loved to kick his boots through the piles of red and gold and orange leaves. He felt there was something wild and exciting in the wind. It made him want to jump on a horse and gallop for miles, all the way to the edge of the sky and farther.

Best of all, he knew that fall meant crispy spareribs and sweet cider and hot roasted potatoes with melting butter and all the pumpkin pie he could eat. Almanzo could eat a lot of pumpkin pie. He lifted his head and sniffed. It smelled like there would be apple pie tonight. He could eat a lot of apple pie, too.

The only thing he did not like about fall was that it meant the winter was almost here. And this winter was different from the others.

This winter, Almanzo would have to go to the Franklin Academy in Malone.

Almanzo was thirteen years old. His older brother Royal and his older sisters Eliza Jane and Alice had been going to the Academy since they were ten. But Father had kept Almanzo at home on the farm because he needed someone to help with the chores. Almanzo helped his father with the livestock and the horses and everything else around the farm. Father always said he was proud of what a good worker Almanzo was.

He still walked to the regular schoolhouse, a mile and a half away, but he could stay home on days when he was needed. Almanzo liked those days best. He would much rather be out hauling timber or shearing sheep than trapped inside a drafty schoolhouse trying to put sums together or remember the words of the Constitution.

But Mother and Father had decided that this year Almanzo should go with Alice to the Academy. Royal was eighteen now. He was old enough to stay home and help Father on the farm, even though he did not like farming as much as Almanzo did.

Almanzo did not want to go to the Academy. He would have to study his lessons every day. He would have to wear his good suit and sit quietly behind a desk. He would have to share a room with other boys he didn't know. He would have to eat school food, which Alice said was nowhere near as good as Mother's, and you couldn't eat as much as you wanted—only what they served.

But the worst part of all was that he would have to leave his horse, Starlight, who had grown into a beautiful chestnut stallion. There would be no horses at the Academy, only books and slates and stern-looking teachers. It made Almanzo itch to think about it.

He wanted to stay home and work on the farm, but he knew he could not argue with Father. The decision had been made. In a few weeks, Almanzo and Alice would get in the sleigh and be driven off to Malone. Then he probably would not see Starlight again until Christmas.

Almanzo and Father took off their barn smocks and hung them out on the porch. Father scraped his boots on the foot scraper at the door and Almanzo copied him. He set his heel in the curve of the iron curlicue and dragged his boot against the sharp edges to break loose the dirt. His toe knocked against the metal frame on the wall. Almanzo examined his soles carefully before he went inside. Mother didn't like it when they brought dirt from the barn into her clean, well-swept house.

Almanzo could hear Eliza Jane's voice when they opened the door. She was supposed to be helping Mother with the supper, but she always did more talking than cooking. Almanzo washed his hands at the washbasin by the door, drying them on the roller towel. He combed his hair in front of the small mirror. Father went into the dining room, but Almanzo stayed in the warm, bustling kitchen with the smell of sizzling pork.

"Well, I say," Eliza Jane declared, "that it would only be fair." She was stirring a giant pot of something on the stove, while Almanzo's other sister, Alice, was hurrying around the kitchen doing most of the work.

"But I don't know if it's necessary, dear," Mother said without turning around. Almanzo could tell that she was only half-listening to Eliza Jane. "I would only vote the same way as your father, and I'm sure that's true of most women."

"Not me," Eliza Jane said stoutly. "I would vote my own mind, if I could. If they can make one amendment, they should make another." Eliza Jane had been going on for months about the new amendment to the Constitution that let all men vote regardless of the color of their skin. She thought women should be allowed to vote, too.

Alice smiled at Almanzo behind Eliza Jane's back. Her hand whisked something off the table, hiding it in the folds of her apron. As she bustled from one pan to another, she slipped it to Almanzo. He could tell from the warmth and softness that it was a crust of newly baked bread.

This was why Alice was his favorite sister. Alice knew that Almanzo was always starving after chores. He wasn't supposed to eat until everyone else was served, but his stomach was growling loud enough to be heard in Malone.

He took a step back toward the pantry and snuck a bite of the bread. It crunched warm and delicious in his mouth. Eliza Jane turned and looked at him suspiciously. She always seemed to know when he was doing something he shouldn't.

Almanzo's mother was the busiest person he knew. Father sometimes said she worked twice as hard as he did. When she wasn't cooking or gardening or cleaning, she was weaving on her great loom upstairs, or teaching her children something new, or writing to her brothers and sisters who lived far away.

She loved inviting family to visit. Having lots of people to feed and laugh with made her eyes shine and her cheeks pink. That was one reason Almanzo wished it could be Christmas every day—being with all their cousins made his mother so happy. (Most of the other reasons had to do with food.)

Mother stopped and smoothed down a stray lock of his hair. "Thank you for cleaning up so nicely. I am very glad to see you didn't bring any of the barn in here with you."

Eliza Jane tilted up her nose and sniffed as if she were about to disagree.

"Eliza Jane," Mother said. "Take that letter to Father and let him know supper is ready."

Almanzo saw a square of white on the table. Royal must have brought it back from town while he and Father were in the barn.

He stood out of the way of Eliza Jane's bright red hoopskirts as she bustled out with the letter. "Who do you think the letter is from?" he asked Alice.

"It's from Uncle George," she said, lifting a big plate of fried apples'n'onions.

"Alice!" Mother scolded.

"It was on the envelope!" Alice protested. "It said Spring Valley, Minnesota." Their uncle, Mother's youngest brother, had just bought land out west in Minnesota. His new wife, Martha, was the daughter of one of the first pioneers in Spring Valley. His letters were full of stories about the new buildings going up and all the rich open land waiting to be farmed. He sounded very glad to be somewhere that wasn't all settled yet, helping to build a whole new town.

He wasn't the only one. Uncle Charles and Aunt Hannah had written the same thing about their new home in Wisconsin. So had Aunt Phebe and Uncle Joseph. Almanzo's school friend Miles had gone to North Dakota with his family. Sometimes it seemed to Almanzo as if everyone he knew was moving out west.

He wondered what it was like out there, where everything was new and a young man could become any kind of person he wanted. He liked life in Malone, but he didn't have a lot of choices here. He followed in his father's footsteps around the farm and went to school like his mother wanted. If he could invent his own life, what would it be like? What would he want to be, if he could be anything at all?

He knew one thing: He would much rather go west and ride Starlight on the open prairie than go to the Academy and learn sums.

"Almanzo, put this on the table," his mother said, handing him a platter of baked beans. "And mind you be careful with it." The rich, sweet smell of the molasses and brown beans made his insides curl up with hunger. He carried it slowly through the door, watching where he put his feet. He stepped carefully across the cheerful rag-carpet and set the platter in an empty space on the crisp white tablecloth.

Father was already sitting at the head of the table. He was reading the letter, holding it close to the lamp. His beard was not as long or as brown as it used to be. Now it was a square tuft on his chin with gray hairs in it. But his blue eyes still twinkled, and he stood as tall and strong as Royal. He had sons and hired men to help him, but he loved farmwork, and he did as much as he could himself. He said he meant to keep working until he was a hundred, and if he had to die then, it would be while he was plowing a field or breaking in a horse.

The envelope was lying on the tablecloth by Father's elbow. Almanzo peeked at it as he adjusted the platter of baked beans. In one corner was a blue three-cent postage stamp with a picture of a train puffing merrily across it.

Almanzo thought about how exciting it would be to get on that train and ride all the way out to Minnesota.

Eliza Jane was walking around the dining room with the baby in her arms. Everyone had been surprised when Mother had another baby twelve years after Almanzo. Father said he was a blessing, and they named him Perley.

Almanzo thought he was a very funny baby. Perley grinned and gurgled at everyone and everything, especially the horses and the cows and the cats. He sucked on his own fingers and then tried to put other people's fingers in his mouth, too. His eyes always got very big when he ate, as if he were as happy about food as Almanzo was. He would grab the spoon, throw it in the air, look surprised when it disappeared, and then flap his hands for more.

Almanzo hadn't known that babies could be funny before Perley came along. He couldn't wait until Perley was big enough to walk and talk, so Almanzo could be a real big brother to him, like Royal was to Almanzo.

Perley's hair was shiny and soft, glowing gold in the lamplight. He wrinkled his nose and tried to push away from Eliza Jane, but she was holding him too tightly. Almanzo guessed that Eliza Jane was just as curious about the letter as he was. She was using Perley as an excuse to stay in the dining room, in case Father said something about Uncle George. But it was almost Perley's bedtime, and the baby was not happy about being bounced around the dining room. He let out a piercing shriek, like a very loud wild bird, and wriggled unhappily in his sister's arms. Father looked up with a frown.

"Eliza Jane," he said, "perhaps it is time for Perley to go to bed."

Eliza Jane sighed. "Yes, Father." She carried Perley out to his crib in their parents' room, a small space just off the dining room. Almanzo heard her singing the baby a lullaby as he finished setting the table. Some nights Perley wanted to stay up and play for hours, but tonight he must have fallen asleep quickly, since Eliza Jane soon came out and went into the kitchen again.

Finally Mother and Alice and Eliza Jane came in with the rest of the supper—roasted golden squash and fluffy cornbread, mashed turnips and thick slices of fried pork, speckled strawberry preserves for the newly baked bread and spicy apple pie with a sweet pastry crust.

Almanzo forgot about the letter as he watched the food being laid out. He waited while Father said the blessing and served all the others first. One day, when Perley could sit at the table with them, he would be the youngest and he would be served last instead of Almanzo. Then Almanzo would tell him stories about the farm and sound very grown up, the way Royal did.

It wasn't until they had been eating in silence for a while that Father brought up the letter.

"George sounds very happy in Spring Valley," he said thoughtfully to Mother. "The more I think on it, the more I wonder if going west might be a good idea for ourselves, too."

Almanzo felt a leaping flutter in his chest.

He'd never thought they might actually join the pioneers who were building a new country out west. Was it possible?

"But James," Mother said, "we're doing well here. The farm is prosperous, and we have so many friends. Why would we leave?"

Father tugged on his beard. "The farm is not as prosperous as it once was," he said. "The hop crops have been weak for the last couple of years. Everyone says the best investments are out west, where the land is clear and unspoiled."

Mother did not look convinced. Almanzo took a forkful of roasted squash and blew on it to cool it down. Eliza Jane gave him one of her scandalized looks, but he ignored her.

"We would be closer to Hannah and Phebe and George," Father pointed out. "Everyone seems to be thinking of moving west. Perhaps it would be best to go before the whole family leaves us behind."

"I do miss George," Mother said. He was her youngest brother, and she had helped raise him. In her stories about him, George was always funny, curious, and mischievous. He was the first to take a dare or explore a new place. It was not surprising that he had gone west to find his wife and a place to live. "But we would have to leave Andrew and Sarah, and Wesley . . ."

"Unless they decide to move west as well," Father said. "And if we are going to move, we should do it before any of the children are settled, so that they can all come with us."

Almanzo's heart was beating so hard he was sure everyone at the table could hear it. Imagine going west instead of attending the Academy! Perhaps his dream of riding Starlight across the prairie might really come true.

Alice looked excited, too. Only Royal looked disappointed. Almanzo could guess why. Royal wanted to be a storekeeper. He had been working as an apprentice in the grocery store in town this summer. Moving west meant working on a farm all the time, which Royal did not like as much as Almanzo and Father did.

Maybe that was in Father's mind, too. He always said that Royal was a grown man and would soon be making his own decisions. But Almanzo knew that Father thought being a farmer was the proudest and best work a man could do. Perhaps he hoped that taking Royal west would make Royal want to be a farmer.

Almanzo thought again about all the different things a young man could do if he were building a new life for himself. Would he still want to be a farmer if his father let him choose his own path? He could not imagine wanting to be a storekeeper like Royal did.

"Well, I think we should start by visiting," Father said. He took the letter out of his vest pocket and put it on the table beside Mother's plate. "George has invited us to stay, so we can meet Martha and see what Spring Valley is like. I think he would like us to see his new farm."

Mother's mouth was a little round "O" of surprise. "But—when?" she asked. She touched the letter but did not pick it up. "And what about our farm?"

"We would only go for a short time . . . a few months, perhaps, to understand the land and see the town before we make any decisions," Father said. "We could leave Royal in charge here, with Eliza Jane and Almanzo to help him."

Almanzo felt like big stones were clunking down inside his chest. He wouldn't get to go west after all. He'd have to stay here and get bossed around by his older brother and sister. It would be very strange to have the family split up for months. He remembered the time when he was younger and Father and Mother left them alone while they went to visit Uncle Andrew. Almanzo and his brother and sisters made ice cream and pulled candy and had a wonderful time.

But that was only for a week, and as they got older, Royal became more serious and Eliza Jane got even more bossy. He would not want to be left behind with her in charge . . . especially not for *months*!

"Perley would come, of course," Mother said.

"But what about Alice? And isn't Almanzo a bit young to be left without us?"

Almanzo was *not* young. He was full thirteen years old and just as useful around the farm as any of the men Father hired. He dared not interrupt his parents to say so, but he thought it with all his might. They should take him with them, not because he was young, but because he would be useful out west, too!

The glimmering lamplight reflected off their faces around the table. Everyone was eating very quietly, as if they did not want to distract Mother and Father from this important conversation. The dining room seemed small and cozy and very familiar. Almanzo could picture every bit of it with his eyes closed. He knew where every book was placed, every seashell and every piece of pretty fabric. He knew the pattern woven in the rag-carpet and the picture of George Washington on the wall. He knew the view from the windows at every time of the year. Nothing had changed very much in the thirteen years he had been alive.

He had never thought about it changing.

But now it felt too small and too much the same. He wanted something new. He wanted a place he could help build with his own hands. He wanted to see faces he had never seen before, and a prairie that stretched all the way to the sky with no end in sight.

"I suppose Alice could stay here, too," Father said, tugging on his beard again. Alice couldn't hide the look of disappointment on her face.

"Almanzo is supposed to begin at the Academy this year," Mother reminded him.

Father turned his twinkling eyes to Almanzo. "That is true. I know how much you were looking forward to that, Manzo."

"No, sir!" Almanzo burst out. He caught himself quickly. "I mean—yes, sir. But—that is—it seems to me that there could be a lot to learn from traveling. Maybe as much as I could learn from a classroom full of books. Maybe even more. And I could help around Uncle George's farm and take care of the horses and do anything that would be useful, sir."

"Hmm," Father said. The corners of his mouth twitched up in a small smile. "You make a powerful argument. But you realize we would be leaving Starlight here, and we cannot be sure how long we will be gone."

Almanzo's forkful of turnips stuck in his throat. Leave Starlight behind—and not just until Christmas, but for who knows how many months? Anything could happen while they were gone. They might have to stay in Minnesota for longer than anyone expected. Starlight might forget about Almanzo and all his careful training.

"What do you think, Alice?" Mother asked.

"I want to go with you," Alice said. "If I may say so. You could use my help with Perley, couldn't you, Mother?" Almanzo guessed she was thinking that if she had to stay here and be bossed around by Eliza Jane, Alice would end up walking all the way to Minnesota just to get away from her.

"Well, Almanzo?" Father asked. "Stay here with Starlight and help Royal run the farm? Or leave Starlight and come west with us?"

"Or go to the Academy as we planned," Mother put in.

Almanzo rubbed his forehead, thinking hard. It was not often that Father asked his opinion on such big matters. This was a decision that could change everything for Almanzo.

He knew he did not want to go to the Academy. He knew he would love to see Spring Valley and all the wide open land out west. But he would be terribly sad to leave Starlight, no matter how long they were gone.

He looked across the table at Alice, who widened her eyes at him. This was also a choice between Alice, whom he liked, and Eliza Jane, who was difficult. But then he'd also be leaving Royal. Almanzo was always lonelier when Royal was away at the Academy. What would the family be like without Royal or Eliza Jane?

Father was waiting for an answer. Almanzo looked into his eyes and squared his shoulders. He didn't want to stay just because it was less scary than going. He wanted to make the brave choice, the exciting choice—the choice that would make his life more remarkable.

"I want to go with you, too," he said.

Eliza Jane frowned, but Father's smile was as big as Almanzo had ever seen. "Let's give it a try, Angeline," Father said, taking Mother's hand. "Let's see what we think of Spring Valley. It's only a visit. We can always come back here if it seems wrong for us."

"Whatever you think best, James," Mother agreed.

"We shall take Alice and Almanzo with us," Father said. "If nothing else, it will be an adventure for us all."

Alice bounced a little in her seat and Eliza Jane gave her a stern look. Almanzo bent his head and grinned across the beans at Alice.

Almanzo was going west!

A SAD FAREWELL

It took a long time to prepare for their trip. Almanzo was glad that his work kept him in the barn, out of the way of Mother and Eliza Jane. Mother was in a constant flurry of cleaning and packing and mending. Almanzo had not thought she could get any busier than before, but she did. Alice complained that she had never had to do so much sewing in all her born days.

But it was important that they have everything they would need in Spring Valley. Mother seemed to think that they would not be able to get any new supplies out west. Father laughed and said the trains would still come and they would not be far from a general store. But Mother set her mouth firmly and kept packing.

One day in January, soon after Almanzo's fourteenth birthday, Mother called Almanzo to carry a trunk up to his room. He had never seen it before. The sides were made of smooth, solid brown wood, glossy like Starlight's coat. Four brass bands ran around it from the top to the bottom, gleaming a shiny yellow in the sunshine. Almanzo ran his fingers over the domed brass studs, as big as his fists. He knelt to look at the lock.

There was a small iron keyhole in a metal plate on the front. It was covered by a keyhole cover that swung from side to side like the pendulum on the tall clock in the hall. The cover was shiny like the brass bands, with a tiny bird carved in it. The bird had a hooked beak and wide-stretched wings, like the eagles in Almanzo's schoolbooks.

It was one of the most handsome trunks Almanzo had ever seen. He could imagine the woodworkers making it. He thought of them smoothing down the pine boards and fitting together the corners and hammering wooden slats into the top to keep it sturdy. There was a curve in the middle of the trunk that must have been difficult to carve so that all the sides still matched. He wished he had the skill to make a trunk like this. Perhaps if they moved out west, one day he might become a woodworker.

"Almanzo, do you know what this is?" Mother asked. She touched the smooth brown wood with a smile.

Almanzo wasn't sure what to say. "Isn't it a trunk?"

"It's a Jenny Lind trunk," Mother said. "Do you know who Jenny Lind is?"

Almanzo racked his brain. Was she someone he should have learned about in school? He could not remember the name "Jenny Lind" from his history lessons. He worried that he was going to get in trouble for forgetting. If

Mother thought that he had not been studying enough, she might make him stay home and go to the Academy.

He looked down at the trunk. If the trunk was named after Jenny Lind, perhaps she was someone who had to travel a lot. He tried to think of famous women who traveled.

"Was she married to a president?" he guessed.

Mother laughed, and Almanzo felt his shoulders relax. She was not angry.

"No, Jenny Lind is a singer," Mother said. "The most beautiful singer who ever lived. They call her the 'Swedish Nightingale.'"

"She's from Sweden?" Almanzo said.

"Yes, but she came to America a long time ago," Mother said, "before Royal was born. She did a tour here, singing concerts in many cities, and she gave much of the money to charity. She has a good soul and the voice of an angel."

Mother's pretty blue eyes were shining. She seemed to be seeing something else in the air behind Almanzo. He looked over his shoulder, then looked back at her.

"Did you hear her sing, Mother?" he asked.

Mother gave a little start, as if she had forgotten he was there. She patted her smooth brown hair and smiled. "Yes," she said. "Your father took me all the way to New York City for her concert. It cost a great deal of money, but it was the most wonderful day." She closed her eyes and sang:

> *"For song has a home in the hearts of the free!*
> *And long as thy waters shall gleam in the*
> *sun,*
> *And long as thy heroes remember their scars.*
> *Be the hands of thy children united as one,*
> *And peace shed her light on thy banner of*
> *stars."*

Almanzo was amazed. He had only ever heard his mother sing in church, or little nursery rhymes to Perley. Her voice was high and sweet—perhaps not a nightingale, but pretty enough to him.

"I'll never forget that," Mother said. "That was Jenny's song about coming to America."

"I wish I could have seen her," Almanzo said. More than that, he wished he could have gone to New York City. It sounded like an exciting place. He thought it was probably too crowded to live in, but it would be interesting to visit and see how everyone lived packed in together, with hundreds of strangers arriving on tall ships from faraway lands every day.

"This is the kind of trunk she used," Mother said, "and so people here started to make them, too, and now they are called Jenny Lind trunks." She sounded brisk and busy again, the way she usually did. The dreamy look had left her face, although her eyes were still bright with memories. "Be careful with it, Almanzo; we have had it for years without scratching it. Take it upstairs to your room. We will pack your things and Alice's in it."

Almanzo lifted the trunk by the leather handles on each end. It was wide and hard for him to turn around the stairs, but he got it to his room without bumping it into the walls. It was also very heavy. He didn't know if he'd be able to lift it once it was full.

In the room he shared with Royal, Almanzo knelt and opened the trunk with the little brass key his mother had given him. The inside was covered in a flowery paper, decorated with green vines of small pink and purple and white flowers. It looked like one of his sisters' sprigged muslin dresses. He wished it were a print of horses instead. But when the trunk was shut, no one would see the flowers.

He closed the trunk again and sat on it, thinking. Now the move seemed more real than ever. He wanted to start throwing his clothes into the trunk right away, but he knew his mother wouldn't be pleased if he did that. She liked to plan carefully before packing anything. He would have to wait for her to tell him how she wanted it.

The winter was almost over by the time they were ready to leave. Melting snow was dripping from the bare apple trees. There were large, icy mud puddles all across the ground and in the road and around the house. No one could tell how deep they were by looking at them. Brown splatters covered Almanzo's boots and pant legs by the end of every day. The horses shied away from the puddles and made scornful blowing sounds, lifting their feet daintily as if they wanted to keep them dry.

The day before they were to leave, Almanzo went to say good-bye to Starlight.

He was very sad about leaving his beautiful horse. Starlight was the first colt Almanzo had raised, with Father's help. Working with Starlight, Almanzo had learned how to treat horses with gentle firmness and how to guide them to obey him without breaking their spirit.

When Starlight was four years old, Father had asked if Almanzo wanted to sell him. He was a beautiful stallion, with a quick pace, a glossy coat, and an elegant stance. And he was a Morgan horse, which was a highly regarded breed. Almanzo could easily have sold Starlight for two hundred dollars, maybe even three hundred.

But Almanzo had decided not to sell him. He planned to spend many years riding Starlight around the farm. He dreamed that perhaps one day Starlight would be the first horse in his own stable.

Now he had to leave Starlight behind, and he did not know when he would see the stallion again. They were going by train to Minnesota, so they could not bring any horses or livestock with them. Father was not sure how long they would be there. They would have to see what they thought of Spring Valley before they made up their minds about moving.

"Don't worry, Manzo," Royal said, coming into the barn with a bucket of water from the well. "I will take good care of Starlight while you're gone."

"I know you will," Almanzo said. He stroked Starlight's soft, velvety nose. The horse nickered quietly and leaned into Almanzo's palm. His large brown eyes watched every move Almanzo made. They were gentle and understanding, as if Starlight knew that Almanzo had to leave, but he was sad about it, too. His long black mane hung down, silky smooth. Almanzo always took care to groom Starlight perfectly every day. His coat shone like polished copper.

"Don't forget to brush him in strong circles," Almanzo said. "He likes a firm hand on the currycomb. And if he doesn't like something, first he will lash his tail back and forth, and then his ears will lay back, and then you'd better get out of the way." Starlight had a gentle disposition, but he was proud and strong, and Almanzo had been knocked into the stable wall a few times before he had learned how to spot Starlight's moods.

"Well, I am considerable older than you be," Royal said, setting down the bucket, "and I reckon I've brushed down a horse before."

"He has a spot right here that tickles him," Almanzo said, pointing to the front of one of

Starlight's long, well-muscled legs. "So be careful when you groom him there, because he hates that. And his favorite thing is carrots, so give him lots of those, but don't spoil him."

"Manzo!" Royal threw up his hands. "I know how to care for horses! Do you think working in a store has turned my mind to molasses?"

Maybe, Almanzo thought. He was sure that Royal thought more about the price of wheat than he did about how best to exercise a horse. And the wrong kind of handling could wreck Almanzo's careful training. Starlight wasn't like any other horse; he was special and noble and had to be treated the right way.

Royal went on. "If Father thinks I can run this place fine while you're gone, it seems to me that you should think the same."

"I do," Almanzo said. "I know." He kicked his boots in the straw. "Just—don't let Eliza Jane ride him or drive him, all right?"

Royal's expression changed. He put one hand on Almanzo's shoulder. His hand was

much bigger than Almanzo's, strong and cal-
lused from work even though he had been in
a store so much this year. It felt like Father's
hand, telling Almanzo without words not to
worry.

"I promise you," Royal said. "I will take
the best care of your horse while you are gone,
Manzo." He grinned. "And if Eliza Jane tries
to go near him, I'll tell her how much he likes
to be tickled right there."

Almanzo laughed. "Do you want to come
riding with us?" he asked. "Father said I could
take Starlight for one last gallop." He stroked
Starlight's nose again. Father did not talk a lot
about his own childhood, but sometimes he
mentioned a colt he'd trained named Thunder.
Almanzo's grandfather Abel had sold Thunder
without giving Father a choice. Father said it
was the right thing to do—he had nine brothers and sisters, and the family needed every
penny they could get.

Still, Almanzo knew he was lucky Father
let him make his own decisions about Starlight.

He thought perhaps Father remembered Thunder and understood how Almanzo felt.

Royal hurried away to saddle his favorite horse, Flame. Almanzo put a light woven blanket on Starlight. Then he brought out his own saddle and slung it over Starlight's back, on top of the blanket. Starlight shook his head and pranced in place. He was as excited as Almanzo about going outside.

Almanzo reached under Starlight's stomach for the long cinch strap and buckled it firmly but not too tightly, securing the saddle in place. He checked to make sure he could slide his fingers between the strap and Starlight's glossy sides. The supple leather of the saddle and straps glowed in the lamplight. Almanzo had spent many hours oiling it and cleaning it to keep the saddle free of dirt and sweat, so that it would not rub against Starlight's back and make him uncomfortable.

Almanzo adjusted the stirrups to the right height and slipped the bridle over Starlight's head. Starlight stood still and accepted the metal bit in his mouth. He was a good horse, and he knew that Almanzo would not pull too hard on the reins or jerk Starlight's head back. He never danced away when Almanzo came up with the bridle, the way some horses did.

Almanzo gathered the reins in his hand and clicked his tongue softly to lead Starlight out of his stall. The stallion's hooves thudded against the straw-covered floor of the barn, and his flanks gleamed as he walked under the lamps.

At the other end of the long barn, Royal was coming toward them, leading Flame. The other horse was a redder brown than Starlight, and whenever he ran it was like fire flickering across the prairie. But Flame was more stubborn than Starlight, and sometimes he would stop to eat leaves off the trees no matter how they coaxed him. Starlight was a much better horse—Almanzo was quite sure of it.

Royal followed Almanzo and Starlight out into the stable yard. Almanzo lifted the reins over Starlight's head and held them in place at the front of the saddle with one hand. Starting on Starlight's left side, he planted his foot in the left stirrup, gripped the back of the saddle with his other hand, and swung himself up to sit on top of the horse.

Starlight looked around at Royal and Flame, as if he were thinking, *Hurry up! What is taking you so long?* In a moment Royal was up in the saddle, and Almanzo gave Starlight the signal to go ahead.

The stallion jumped forward as if he wanted to start running right away, but Almanzo made him walk first, so he could warm up before galloping. At a slow, stately pace, they made their way out of the stable yard into the wide fields behind the barns.

Then Almanzo glanced back at Royal with a grin. As they came to the top of a clear rise, Almanzo leaned forward and touched his heels lightly to Starlight's sides.

Starlight leaped into a gallop, thundering down the hill. His long dark mane and tail went streaming out behind him, and his hooves flashed like lightning below Almanzo. The cold, brisk wind tossed Almanzo's hair and made his eyes water and his throat sting as he laughed. He felt like he could keep riding Starlight right into the sky.

They reached the stand of trees at the far end of Father's land long before Royal and Flame did. Almanzo trotted Starlight in a circle for a few minutes, watching the horse's breath puff out in little clouds around his nose.

When Royal caught up, they swung down from the saddles and sat on the tree roots. Almanzo pulled two apples out of his pockets and gave one to his brother.

"I wish you could come with us," Almanzo said. "I wish we could just move out west right now with you and Starlight and all of us together." He thought for a minute. "Well, maybe Eliza Jane could stay here."

"I wonder what the stores are like in Spring Valley," Royal said thoughtfully. He rubbed his chin, where he was trying to grow a beard. Nothing had come in yet but little bits of brown fuzz that were lighter than the hair on his head. "There must be a good business in selling supplies to the farmers out there, as long as the trains keep coming in."

"A good farm doesn't need a lot of supplies," Almanzo said stoutly. "Father says a good farmer can take care of himself. He can live off the earth. He is as independent as he wants to be."

"Yes, unless the crops fail," Royal pointed out. "Or if the weather is bad, or wolves eat your sheep, or your cows catch a disease, or a prairie fire takes all your wheat." He shook his head. "A lot of things can go wrong in a farmer's life. But people always need storekeepers—even farmers. That is why storekeepers are usually the richest men in town."

"Maybe they are," Almanzo said, "but I would rather work in the open air with horses and crops than do sums and order supplies and bargain with customers all day."

"Well, you can have your farm," Royal said, "and then you can ride into town and buy your supplies from me."

"And then *you* can come out for Christmas dinner and eat the pig I raised and the bread made from my own wheat and all the vegetables I've grown on my own land."

"It's a good thing you invited good old Uncle Royal," Almanzo's brother teased, "or else where would your children get their Christmas candy? You can't grow *that* on a farm, little brother."

"Children!" Almanzo said with a laugh. He shivered his shoulders as if cold water were running down his back. "First I'd have to find a wife!"

"Best of luck with that," Royal said. "Especially since all the pretty girls will be terribly in love with your handsome, rich, storekeeper brother instead."

"Only the boring girls," Almanzo said. "The ones who like counting boxes and doing maths."

"You mean the ones who like having everything they could ever want," Royal said. "Such as sleeping on store-bought sheets and letting their maidservants bring them tea in bed."

"If my wife couldn't get out of bed to make her own tea," Almanzo said, "then I'd think she was a bit of a goose."

"Not much of a romantic, are you, Manzo?" Royal said with a grin.

"Race you home," Almanzo said, jumping up. "Whoever gets there first will marry the prettiest girl."

"Hey!" Royal said, scrambling to his feet. "That's not fair!" But Almanzo was already in the saddle and turning Starlight to gallop away. He heard Royal shouting behind him and laughed again. He leaned forward and rubbed Starlight's neck, stretched out and gleaming as the horse raced over the muddy ground.

"I'll miss you, Starlight," he whispered. "But I promise we'll come back soon—and then I'll take you out west, where we will run and run and run all the way to the end of the sky."

RIDING THE RAILROAD

At last the day of their departure arrived. Almanzo could hardly sleep the night before they were to leave. He kept turning over in the bed, pulling the blanket around, until Royal made a grumpy sleepy noise. Then Almanzo tried to lie still. He stared up at the dark ceiling, listening to the drip-drip of melting ice on the roof. He thought about how strange it would be to sleep in a bed without Royal next to him. He would have no one to talk to about his day on the farm. The bed had always felt big and empty while Royal was away at the Academy. Almanzo would have to get used to sleeping alone all over again.

He thought about whether he had everything he needed in his trunk. He thought about how quickly he would dress in the morning. He worried that he might sleep too long and make them all late for the train, even though he knew Mother would never let that happen.

He could not imagine what he might see out west. This would be his first train ride, and it would take many days to get to Minnesota. They would have to sleep on the train. How strange that would be!

He wondered what kind of horses there were in Minnesota. Surely none would be so fine as Starlight. For the hundredth time he wondered how long they would be gone, and how long it would be before he saw Starlight again. Almanzo knew that Mother thought they would be home by the end of the summer, but Father wanted to wait and decide once they were in Spring Valley.

His eyes began to ache, and he thought that he would never fall asleep. But then he blinked, and when he opened his eyes again, a faint, pale light was coming through the window. So he must have slept a little, although he felt just as wide awake as before.

He strained his ears and heard movement downstairs. Father was getting up to do the last chores before leaving. The rope strings under the mattress creaked as Almanzo got out of bed. He wanted to help Father in the stable, but all of his clothes were packed except for the fine suit he had to wear on the train.

Careful and quiet, trying not to wake Royal or the girls in the next room, Almanzo broke the ice in the bowl of water on the dresser. He scrubbed his face, shivering as the freezing drops touched his skin. Quickly and quietly, he wet his hair and combed it down.

He pulled on his stiff, dark wool trousers and his pressed white shirt and his neat gray vest. He buttoned the shirt with fumbling cold fingers in the dark, starting from the bottom so he could be sure to line up the right buttons with the right buttonholes. He laced up the new black boots the cobbler had made him in the fall. He pulled on his short coat and dropped his jackknife and comb in one of the pockets. He took his new boughten cap from the hook on the door and fitted it snugly on his head. Then he looked around the room one last time. He had everything he needed from here. Leaving this bedroom was like leaving behind a pair of too-small boots.

Almanzo crept down the narrow wooden stairs into the family room. Mother was stoking the kitchen fire. Father was standing by the door, and he looked up as Almanzo came in. The tall clock said it was half-past four.

"Couldn't sleep?" Father said with a smile. Almanzo shook his head.

"I'd like to help with the chores," he said.

"Not in your nice clothes," Mother said. "Royal will be up soon. He can do them. He'll have to manage them by himself when we're gone."

"French Joe and Lazy John will help him when he needs it," Father said. He looked down at Almanzo and stroked his beard. His eyes were twinkling. "Perhaps Almanzo could just follow me around the stables, Angeline. I'll make sure he doesn't roll in any hay."

Almanzo held his breath until his mother finally nodded. "But you be very careful, Almanzo James Wilder! I don't want to get on that train with my son looking like a ragged hobo."

"Thank you, Mother!" Almanzo said. He tugged on the woolly gray mittens that Alice had knitted for him last Christmas and followed Father out to the barn to say good-bye to everything.

He said good-bye to the Big Barn Floor, piled high with hay to the pointed roof up above. He said good-bye to the hog pens and the calf pens and the threshing floor in the South Barn. He said good-bye to the sheep that huddled together for warmth in the sheepfold. He said good-bye to the haymows and the pitchforks hung along the wall. He said good-bye to his two strong oxen, Star and Bright, with their warm brown eyes and thick red fur and curved horns.

He said good-bye to the Buggy-House and the henhouse, and last of all he said good-bye to the Horse-Barn, where all the beautiful horses stuck their heads out of the stalls to see him off. He was old enough now to rub their smooth foreheads and run his hands back along their warm curved necks into their thick manes. But he could not get too close. If Mother found horsehairs on his good suit, he knew she would be very cross.

Of course, he still let Starlight bury his warm nose in his hands. He slipped his horse one last piece of carrot before he left. He hoped Starlight would remember him for all the long months that Almanzo would be gone.

As he went back from the barn up the side path to the house, he passed Royal going to the stables. Royal looked sleepy and his hair was rumpled, as if he hadn't been awake enough to smooth it properly.

Back in the house, breakfast was ready. There was a platter of Mother's wonderful fluffy buckwheat pancakes, stacked and spread with golden butter and covered in sweet molasses. There were fried sausages and onions, sizzling brown with a mouthwatering smell. There were finely hashed brown potatoes with a perfect crunchy crust. There were warm biscuits that broke apart like clouds and thick blueberry preserves to spread on them. And there was plenty of hot tea, smelling like summer wind and warming Almanzo down to his toes.

Everyone was awake now. Eliza Jane told Almanzo twice to straighten his collar and three times not to kick his chair, even though he was sure he was doing no such thing. Because they had to leave for the train station so early, they did not wait for Royal, although he joined them halfway through the meal.

Baby Perley could tell that everyone was excited about something, but he was too little to understand what was happening. He banged his spoon on the table until Eliza Jane took it away, and then he cried until she gave it back. Mother and Alice fussed over Perley, trying to feed him and keep him clean, which were two jobs that did not go together very well.

Almanzo ate steadily until he was full, and then he ate a little more just in case, until he felt stuffed like a bolster pillow. It might be a long time until they ate again. He hoped very much that they were allowed to eat on the train.

At last Royal brought the buggy with the red wheels around and helped load the trunks into it. There was one trunk for Mother and Father and the Jenny Lind trunk for Alice and Almanzo. Mother had a separate satchel for Perley's baby things. Almanzo was happy to see her give Alice a covered dinner pail to carry. Perhaps they would not starve on the train after all.

In Almanzo's satchel he had a change of clothes, his spare comb, and a reader, which his mother had made him pack so he could study on the train. Almanzo hoped she would forget about it in the excitement of riding the railroad.

There was not enough room for all their luggage and all of them in the buggy, so Eliza Jane had to stay at home. It felt most peculiar to say good-bye to his sister, knowing he was going off on a great adventure and she had to stay at home. It was hard to imagine what life would be like without Eliza Jane's bossing.

Almanzo was almost sorry to leave her, until she said: "Now, Manzo, don't forget to mind your manners, no matter how ill bred the boys are out west. Study hard and write to me often, and for goodness' sakes don't spend all your time with horses, or no one will go near you for the smell." She straightened his collar again, and then she licked her finger to smooth down his hair, but he ducked away before she could.

Eliza Jane was seventeen, and she was going to be a schoolteacher. She had already taken the proper exams to get her certificate.

Almanzo was sure Eliza Jane would like teaching school. There she would be able to boss everyone around. No one would be allowed to talk back to her. She would probably start every day by straightening all the boys' collars and making the girls sit up straight. There would be no fidgeting and no fun. He would not want to be in Eliza Jane's school!

She stood at the door of the red-painted house and waved and waved as they drove away. Almanzo twisted around to look back until Eliza Jane was just a dot in the distance, and then the trees and hills came up to hide the house and he could no longer see his sister or the barns or the place he had lived his whole life.

Father drove the horses with ease, handling them lightly. Sometimes he handed the reins to Royal so he could watch how Royal managed the team. Almanzo was proud to see that Royal did not make any mistakes. He seemed as confident and strong as Father, riding up on the seat with the shining horses pricking their ears and trotting along in front of him.

As they drove along, Mother talked to Perley about what they could see in the farms and fields along the road. He sat on her lap, looking around with wide eyes. The baby was always quiet when Mother spoke, as if he were trying hard to understand her strong, lively voice. It made Almanzo quieter, too, listening to her. It was funny to think that she had sung the same songs and told the same stories to him when he was a baby.

In Malone they drove past the church sheds and straight up to the railroad station by the Square. Although it was early morning, there were already people in the train station, sitting on the benches or standing in line to buy tickets. Almanzo was allowed to hold the horses while Father and Royal unloaded the trunks. Then Father and Mother went into the station to buy the train tickets.

"Well," Royal said awkwardly, "you'll be back 'fore long, I reckon."

"It's not a farewell forever," Alice said, "only

a farewell for now." She hugged baby Perley to her and looked like she was about to cry.

"That's right," Almanzo said. "We'll all be together in Minnesota soon."

"Or back here," Royal said, "if Father thinks it will be too risky to start a farm out there."

Almanzo stuck out his hand and Royal took it. "Good luck, Royal," Almanzo said. "Maybe you'll find that you like being a farmer after all."

Royal patted Perley's head and shook Alice's hand, too, with a solemn air. "Be good," Alice said. "Try to eat something besides ice cream all the time."

Royal laughed. "I'll be amazed if Eliza Jane lets me have any ice cream at all."

"Don't let her boss you too much," Alice said. "You're the oldest."

"I know," Royal said with a grin, "but she'll be the one cooking!"

"That's true. He'll have to stay on her good side," Almanzo agreed. Alice laughed, and he was pleased to see that his teasing had driven away her tears.

Father and Mother came back and said their farewells to Royal. They all stood back with their trunks and watched as Royal swung up into the buggy and the horses trotted away down the street. Their chestnut flanks gleamed in the rising sun and their wild black manes flew out behind them. Royal looked small and alone in the buggy without the rest of the family packed in with him.

Almanzo saw that Perley had fallen asleep in Mother's arms. While they were away, Almanzo would be the big brother of the family. Perley might not even remember Royal when they saw him again. Almanzo hoped he would be as good a brother as Royal was. He reached over and tucked Perley's knitted blue scarf closer around his neck, and Mother smiled at him.

The morning sunshine cast a pale yellow light over the buildings around the Square. Dew sparkled on the grass in the center area, and dust rose in shimmering puffs over the road where Almanzo had watched so many

Independence Day parades. High above them, the American flag fluttered, bright and proud as always, against the blue-gray-pink sky.

Soon the train came whistling in, making an almighty squealing and huffing and grumbling noise. A porter in a dark blue uniform with shiny buttons helped Father and Almanzo lift the trunks on board. The steps of the train car were very high up. Even Father had to use the step-box the porter set out on the ground for the passengers.

Alice took Perley while Mother settled their satchels, but the baby didn't wake up. Then Mother and Alice sat in one seat with Perley, and Father and Almanzo sat in the seat behind them, facing forward. Father let Almanzo sit by the window, which was tall and ran along the whole side of the train, letting in wide bars of bright sunlight so all the brass railings gleamed.

Father sat back and pulled out a newspaper he had bought inside the train station. Soon he was shaking his head and murmuring to himself, as he often did when he read the news. Almanzo put his face up close to the glass of the window and tried to look down to the wheels and tracks of the train far below him. He had seen the crisscrossing railroad tracks many times before, but he had never thought about how a train stayed on them.

Slowly, with a great rumble and a cough of dark gray smoke, the train lurched forward. Flecks of black soot and tiny sparks of floating fire drifted in through a window that was open near the front of the car. Almanzo watched one of the sparks dance closer. He wondered if it would burn a hole in the wooden seats when it landed, but it flared out before it touched anything.

He heard Alice cough, and Mother gave her a handkerchief to hold in front of her face. The air smelled smoky and sharp, tingling and pressing against the back of his throat. It was like the inside of the blacksmith's shop in Malone, where Almanzo had sometimes gone with Father to watch them make horseshoes.

He loved to see the hard, cold metal become a fierce glowing golden red, until it could be beaten and molded into a new shape. He liked the clanging sound of the hammer hitting the iron, and the long arm of the tongs holding the horseshoe over the anvil. He liked the hiss of steam when the finished horseshoe was dropped in water.

Out west, he could become a blacksmith one day if he wanted to. But he would never want to be a blacksmith. Blacksmiths were stuck inside by a hot fire all day long, instead of out in the air like farmers. They were always covered in soot, so much that they could not get their hands clean. They smelled like fire and dirty coins. He was glad there were people in the world who wanted to be blacksmiths, because he was not one of them.

He looked around the car. A smartly dressed older couple was sitting at the far end. The woman had deep wrinkles in her face and thin white hair, and she wore a bonnet with little yellow flowers woven into it. She did not look pleased to be there. She sat staring straight ahead and did not say one word to her husband. He did not look at her either. He clenched a pipe between his teeth and kept his hands folded over his middle. A gold pocketwatch chain ran into one of his vest pockets. Almanzo hoped that when he was that old, he would have more to say to his wife, and that she would look happier to be with him than they did.

Mother and Father talked to each other all the time—about the business of the farm, or the new books Alice brought home from the Academy, or President Ulysses S. Grant, or the letters they got from Almanzo's aunts and uncles. Father often made Mother laugh with stories about the horses, and she made him laugh with stories about Perley.

Three businessmen in suits and hats were across the aisle from Father and Almanzo. The youngest was sitting alone, and he kept leaning forward to talk to the other two. Almanzo thought the older two did not seem very interested in what the youngest had to say. He knew what that was like. Eliza Jane never listened to Almanzo. She was too busy bossing him. Royal listened better, but he did an awful lot of bossing, too.

Neither of them would be able to tell him what to do when he was all the way in Spring Valley!

Outside the window, the town of Malone disappeared quickly, and soon the train was flashing past trees and fields, and then more buildings and another town, and then that disappeared as well.

Almanzo ran his fingers along the hard wooden seat underneath him, and then he twisted around to study the whole train car.

Father lowered the newspaper to look at him. "Did you have a question, son?"

"I was just wondering where we're going to sleep," Almanzo said. "I mean, if we are going to be on this train for days and days—but I don't mind, Father. I can sleep sitting up right here." He straightened his back against the high seat behind him and wondered if that was true. But if Father intended for them to sleep that way, it must be possible.

Father chuckled. "We will not be on this train for days, Almanzo. We have to change trains in Ogdensburg, and then again in Chittenango and again in Buffalo."

"Three times, just in New York?" Almanzo asked.

"That's right," Father said. "But then from Buffalo to Chicago it's one straight shot. We've booked a spot in a Pullman car for that part of the journey, so it'll be just like sleeping in a hotel. You'll see."

Almanzo wanted to ask more questions, but Father had lifted the newspaper once again. So Almanzo contented himself with looking out the window and watching the telegraph poles zip by—*zip! zip!*—like long ribbons against the sky.

They changed trains in Ogdensburg before midday. The new train was bigger, with red velvet seats instead of plain wood, and the ceiling was carved in gold and white painted patterns. Almanzo wished he could see more of the town of Ogdensburg, but all he saw from the train was a lot of big square buildings with painted advertisements on the sides. As they pulled away from the station, he saw a gray horse and rider galloping up one of the main roads, and he felt a pang of missing Starlight.

Mother unwrapped the dinner pail close to noon and shared out the plump slices of ham and soft, nutty bread and crispy doughnuts. She gave them each a handful of dried plums, and their tart sweetness reminded Almanzo of picking them from the thickets in the summer with Alice.

It seemed like a very long day, although Almanzo never got bored with looking out the window at the world rolling by so fast. But at last they pulled into the station at Buffalo and got off the train.

In the glow of the lamps with the darkness pressing against the high windows, the station seemed full of people calling out to greet one another or saying good-bye, checking their tickets, pushing their trunks on wheeled carts, or just sitting and waiting. Almanzo wondered if this was what New York City was like, so crowded and busy all the time.

Alice stayed close to Almanzo, holding Perley tightly in her arms, as they followed Mother and Father through the crowd. Perley was fussier than usual, since it was past his bedtime and he was tired. He would start to cry, stop to yawn, and then go back to crying. Alice bounced him up and down gently, and he buried his face in her neck.

At last Father spotted a familiar face: his cousin Edward, who lived not far outside of Buffalo. Father had written to him that they were coming, and Edward had agreed to meet them and take them to a hotel, as there was not enough room for guests in the place he rented as a bachelor.

Almanzo had never met Edward before, but he liked him right away. He had bright red cheeks and a cheerful smile. Almanzo saw that one of his bootlaces was frayed and tied back together. Edward bowed to Mother and Alice and helped them all into his buggy.

Almanzo's eyes were already drooping as they swayed and clopped through the streets of Buffalo. He barely noticed the doors of the hotel, or the grand lobby with its fine marble walls and large feathery plants. The long day of traveling, and the restless night before of worrying, had caught up to him. He was asleep almost as soon as his head hit the pillow.

A FEW SURPRISES

The next morning they had breakfast at the hotel with Cousin Edward. There were scrambled eggs and fried potatoes and heavy corn muffins that were nowhere near as good as Mother's. Almanzo did not think there was enough to eat. He was still hungry when the plates were cleared away. But he knew he must not complain. At least he did not have chores to do today. He should not get as hungry as he usually did.

Cousin Edward loaded them into his buggy

to take them to the train. Now Almanzo was awake enough to notice Edward's horses. One was dappled light gray with dark spots. Its mane was thick and dark, and Almanzo could see a few knots in it. The other horse was golden yellow like corn. Its ears were always pricked forward and its hindquarters were wide and solid. It moved with a rolling gait, twitching its head from side to side.

They were both good horses, but not as good as Father's horses. Almanzo could see that Cousin Edward had to pull back hard to get them to stop sometimes. If Father had trained them, the horses would know exactly when to stop and stand for him.

They went clop-clopping through the streets of Buffalo, which was the largest city Almanzo had ever been in. The sidewalks were full of well-dressed people hurrying about. Glossy horses and smartly painted buggies trotted up and down the wide roads below the tall brick buildings. Through the windows Almanzo could see men in spectacles sitting at their desks, surrounded by papers. He was glad he was not one of those men. He would hate to be stuck behind a desk all day, breathing the same air all the time, only seeing the sky through a square of glass.

He thought that it must be hard to hear oneself think in a city this big. It was a fine place to visit for some excitement, but it seemed tiring to live there, with noise in the air around you all the time and people in your way wherever you went.

"I bet Royal would like it here," he said to Alice. "He would see all these folks as people who could spend money in his store."

Alice's brown curls were tossed by the wind and her eyes were bright. "It's so busy!" she said. "No one could ever be bored in a big city like this, don't you think?"

"Perhaps," Almanzo said, "but I'd rather have fresh air and space to ride my horses."

Almanzo and Alice saw one row of buildings that had been gutted by fire, with gaping holes in the roof and dark, soot-stained walls open to the sky. A crew of men were busily working to repair the damage. Cousin Edward said that they were the newspaper offices of the *Buffalo Evening Post* and the *Buffalo Courier*, which had caught fire not long ago. Nobody knew why. Almanzo thought it must be very expensive to fix all the machines it took to print a newspaper.

When they got to the train station, Father brought out two sets of tickets. One was to get on the train that would take them all the way from Buffalo to Chicago. The other was for a special car on that train, called a "Pullman car." You needed a separate ticket to ride in this car, which was specially made for sleeping in. It cost more than riding in the regular cars, but since they would be on the train for so long, Father had decided it was worth it to be able to sleep well.

The Pullman cars were painted dark green instead of black like the rest of the train. They were also taller, with windows that opened and closed high up in the car. Father went up to one of the Pullman cars with his tickets and gave them to a stern man in a dark uniform with a smart-looking black cap. The brim of the cap was shiny patent leather like his shoes. There was a silver braid across the front of the cap and a metal badge that said CONDUCTOR on it.

The conductor nodded at Father and gestured to the man next to him. This was the porter, and he was also wearing a uniform, navy wool with a light stripe on the cuff and gleaming buttons. His skin was dark like mahogany, and his hair was cut so close it almost looked shaved. He came forward with a friendly smile, showing his even, bright white teeth, and helped Almanzo lift the trunks into the car. Because Buffalo was a big station, they did not need a step-box here. The station was built with high platforms at the same level as the train stairs.

Father led the way into the Pullman car, followed by Mother and Perley, Alice, and finally Almanzo. The train car was quite as elegant as the hotel room they had stayed in the night before. The floors were carpeted with a gold pattern of vines and leaves against a forest-green background, thick and soft underfoot. Pretty, sparkling glass domes covered the oil lamps hung along the ceiling. Almanzo could feel warm heated air coming through vents along the sides of the floor.

But the strangest thing was that he did not see any beds. The benches were padded and covered in a woolen twill material with a copper-colored checked pattern. Instead of being arranged in rows facing straight ahead, the benches faced each other, so that when Almanzo and Father sat down they could look at Mother and Alice and Perley, who sat facing them. Father said they should let the women face forward, because sometimes riding backward made people dizzy. Almanzo did not think it would make him dizzy. He had ridden on the back of a wagon before; he did not mind seeing the countryside go by in the wrong direction. He was pretty sure it wouldn't make Mother or Alice dizzy either, but he didn't say so.

"Father," he said, "may I ask a question?"

"Yes, son?"

"Where are the beds? I thought we would be sleeping in this car."

"You'll see," Father said with a mysterious smile.

Almanzo sat up straight on the soft velvet of the seats and tried to look important enough to be riding in such a fancy car. He looked out the window and saw a couple walking past to the next Pullman car. They were dressed very elegantly. The man wore a suit with a top hat and a monocle. The lady wore green silk taffeta with a short velvet cape. They walked as if the entire train station belonged to them. They did not even look at the porter as he hurried to carry their bags onto the train.

Father saw where Almanzo was looking. "There are those who can afford private compartments," Father said, "but I think we shall have enough privacy for our needs."

Almanzo peeked over the back of the seat

and saw a man hurry into their car. He had sharp, darting eyes and a stiff, bristly little mustache. He kept licking his lips and pressing his hands together until the knuckles cracked. He barely made it into his seat across the aisle from them before the train started again with a lurch and a shrill whistle.

The whistle woke up Perley, who had fallen asleep for a while, and he began to fuss. He was not used to so much traveling. He did not like having his days so disordered and nothing familiar around him. His blond hair was mussed and his face was red. He kicked and tried to get down so he could crawl around, but Mother kept him firmly on her lap. She sang a little song to him and brought out a toy for him to play with, and soon Perley was distracted with trying to chew on it.

The man across the aisle gave Perley a scornful look, and Almanzo decided right then that he did not like the stranger one bit.

That was another long day. The train stopped many times, at cities big and small, but none so big as Buffalo. Almanzo and Alice played checkers when they got bored of looking out the window, but the game board kept bouncing and sliding their pieces around, so it was hard to keep straight who was winning. Almanzo even tried to study his reader for a while, but he could not concentrate with so much flashing by outside the window.

At noon Father went to the dining car and came back with food wrapped in brown paper—hearty bread and butter and thick slices of juicy ham and crispy apples and golden shortbread biscuits. They ate over white linen napkins on their laps instead of at a table, which made Almanzo feel wonderfully wicked, although he was very careful not to let a single crumb escape him. He had seen the porter go by with a brush, cleaning the car, and he would feel bad if he left a mess for the porter to clean.

There was a silver carafe of water in a little holder at each bench. When each of them had taken a drink, Father called the porter, who took the carafe away to refill it. Almanzo noticed that the porter had taken off his dark wool coat and cap. Inside the car, he wore a white coat of a lighter material. He stayed in the car all the time, and was ready to help whenever a passenger needed him. Almanzo was glad he was there, but he was also sure that he would never want to be a porter.

After they ate, Mother and Father went for a walk along the train and left Perley with Alice and Almanzo for a short while. Perley kept wriggling and reaching for the vine pattern on the carpet. Almanzo set his little feet on the floor of the aisle and held Perley's hands as the baby tottered slowly between the benches. Perley was just learning to walk, and he loved practicing. He beamed and gurgled at all the other passengers, and most of them smiled back at him. It was hard not to smile at Perley's funny toothless grin.

But the man with the stiff mustache still looked disapproving. He watched Perley and Almanzo going back and forth, his small eyes sharp behind his newspaper.

The third time they went past him, the man with the mustache said, "You should be careful."

"Pardon me?" Almanzo said politely.

"Train travel is very dangerous," said the man. "The train could hurtle off the track any minute. I was on a train once that nearly plunged off a cliff into a creek. We could all have been killed." He raised his eyebrows at Perley. "As it was, we were all thrown about like rag dolls in a suitcase."

"Glurr!" Perley said, beaming at the strange man.

Almanzo glanced over and saw that Alice looked pale, although she was staring at her reader and pretending not to listen. "I am sure that this train is very safe," Almanzo said stoutly. "The engineers and the conductor know what they are doing."

"Even if they do," the man said, shaking his head, "sometimes there are terrible accidents no one could foresee. I was just reading about an incident where someone stuck a piece of wood in the switch frog, so when the engine wheels struck it, the train was thrown completely off the track."

"Who would do that?" Almanzo asked, fascinated despite himself.

The stranger opened his eyes very wide. "No one knows," he said. "Some say perhaps bandits intended to attack the train once they'd disabled it. The newspaper called it a dastardly plot. Everyone could have died."

Alice drew in a quick, anxious breath. Perley bounced in Almanzo's hands, eager to keep walking.

"But nobody did die," Almanzo said. "Not that time, or in the accident you were in?"

"Even so," the man said, shaking his head again, "it is a dangerous, dangerous way to travel. People die on trains all the time. Especially when they are not in their seats."

Perley squeaked loudly and tried to pull his hands free so he could keep walking by himself. It was all Almanzo could do to keep a grip on him.

"I thank you for the interesting tales,"

Almanzo said, bending his head to the man. "And I wish you a safe rest of your journey." He hoped that this would prevent the man from talking to him again for the rest of the trip. And indeed, although Almanzo and Perley went by three more times, the stranger with the mustache only sniffed in a chilly way, but said nothing more.

Finally night came. Where were the beds? What would happen now? Father looked at Almanzo with his twinkling eyes, as if he knew how Almanzo's curiosity was fit to bursting out of his chest. Alice was yawning and Perley had already fallen asleep in Mother's lap, his chubby little hands clutching her arm under his cheek as he nestled against her.

The porter got up and went down the car lighting the lamps. He stopped at their end of the car and made a polite little bow to Father.

"Excuse me, sir," he said. "Could I trouble you to move while I make down the beds?"

"Certainly," Father said, folding up his newspaper and picking up the satchels. He moved over to an empty bench, and the others followed him. Perley grumbled softly in his sleep but didn't wake up. "Now watch this, Almanzo," Father said, nodding at the porter. Almanzo perched at the end of the bench to see what would happen.

First the porter stepped between the facing benches and reached up to a part of the wall above them. He undid two leather straps and then, to Almanzo's surprise, a piece attached to the wall leaned out and folded down into a flat bench at about the level of the porter's eyes. On this upper bench was a plain mattress. The porter brought over a step stool and stood on it to make up the bed. He put on starched white cotton sheets and a fluffed-up pillow and a blanket the color of pink sunrises.

Then he went down to the lower benches and worked a mechanism underneath the seats. Almanzo was astonished to see the cushions he had been sitting on all day suddenly slide down. When they met up with the seat across from him, they formed a flat mattress just like the one up top. Then the porter made this into a bed as well, putting on another set of sheets and a matching orange-pink blanket.

"All right," Father said, "it is time to change into our nightclothes."

Almanzo felt a thrill of alarm. "Here? On the train?" he said.

"Oh, I couldn't!" Alice breathed.

"Don't worry," Mother said with a laugh. "This is why we made those dressing gowns you spent so long sewing the hems on."

"Goodness, maybe it was worth it after all, then!" Alice said.

Almanzo followed Father to one end of the car and into a large washroom for the men while Alice and Mother and Perley went to the one for women. Almanzo used the basin of water to scrub his face, which felt as if it was coated in a thick layer of grime. He was not surprised to see how much dirt came off. Although it was not like being in the fields all day, the flecks of soot that came in the ventilation windows had ended up on everyone's skin.

He changed quickly into his long woolen nightshirt and nightcap and pulled on the soft blue wool dressing gown Mother had woven for him. He was glad that Father was there with him, and that no other men came in while they were in there.

When he came back, Alice and Mother were already under the covers in the lower bunk, with Perley tucked snugly between them, fast asleep. Almanzo was happy to see that the porter had hung up a privacy curtain in front of their bunks, along the aisle. After he had climbed up to the upper berth with Father, they were able to draw the curtain and be completely hidden from view. They would not have strangers like the mustache man looking in at them while they slept.

Father set out their shoes to be shined by the porter while they were sleeping, and Almanzo saw that other passengers had done the same. He hoped the porter would not have to stay awake all night shining shoes.

It was a strange, wild feeling to be lying

down in his nightclothes on a train. He could see the moonlit landscape rushing by from where he lay in bed. It made him feel alive and excited. Going west was already a grand adventure, and it was only the second day! He hoped that Spring Valley would be as interesting as the trip to get there.

The rocking of the train was comforting once he got used to it. Sometimes he saw the warm yellow glow of a light in the distance, and he thought about families gathered around their fires, knitting and reading and talking. He thought of all the people who would never go anywhere but the town they were born in, and all the people who were too afraid to move west or go out and see the world.

He was thinking of the people he would meet in Spring Valley, who would all be brave pioneers, when his thoughts began to get muddled and blurry, and his eyes drifted closed. Soon he was deep in slumber, dreaming of trains full of sleeping people in their nightclothes.

SPRING VALLEY

The day they finally arrived in Spring Valley was bright and sunny with a brisk wind to chase away the winter clouds. The platform was bigger and busier than Almanzo had expected. He had imagined a small depot surrounded by miles of open prairie, with almost no one in sight, but there were buildings beyond the station and almost as many people to meet the train as there would have been in Malone.

"It feels like springtime," Almanzo said to Alice as they stepped off the train.

"Perhaps that's why they call it Spring Valley," Alice said with a grin. She turned to look around the depot, tossing her brown curls. Then her face went pink and she looked back at Almanzo with a funny surprised expression.

"Manzo," she whispered, "is that boy over there looking at us?"

Almanzo looked and saw a boy a little older than he was standing at the other end of the platform. The boy had merry brown eyes and brown hair sticking out in unruly tufts from under his cap. He did seem to be looking at Alice, but when he caught Almanzo's eye he grinned and saluted cheekily.

Almanzo was about to wave back when his attention was distracted by someone stepping off the train. It was a girl—the prettiest girl he had ever seen. She had a small turned-up nose and soft brown hair curled in ringlets. She wore a short, pale green cape with a black brocade pattern along the edges and a pink satin lining. On her feet were dainty little boots, and she stepped like Father's Morgan horses, as if she did not want to muddy her shoes on the dirt.

The strange boy jumped forward to help with her luggage, and then two pairs of adults came from either side to join them, greeting one another, and Almanzo could not see the girl anymore.

"Well?" Alice demanded. "Was he looking or not?"

"Oh," Almanzo said, remembering, "oh, yes, I think he was."

"My!" Alice said. "They are forward here in Minnesota, aren't they?"

"Should I start calling you Eliza Jane now?" Almanzo teased, and Alice stuck out her tongue at him.

"Angeline!" a voice cried from the platform. "James!" Mother and Father turned to greet Uncle George as he pressed his way through the crowd. Almanzo would not have recognized him. He had not seen his mother's youngest brother in a few years. He remembered a man with dancing blue eyes like Mother's, a hearty laugh, and a big belly. But now George was much thinner than Father, and he walked with his shoulders lifted, as if he was always cold.

Father stepped forward to shake George's hand, and then he motioned Almanzo forward to shake hands as well. George's smile drooped a little as he saw Almanzo, and then Alice, and then Perley, but all he said was: "Well. Welcome to Spring Valley . . . all of you!"

They followed Uncle George out of the train depot, and Almanzo got his first good look at the town of Spring Valley, Minnesota. It was much smaller than Malone, but much bigger than he'd imagined. From the railroad depot he could see down the street all the way to the prairie, which stretched wide and gold and green and almost treeless for miles. Rolling hills surrounded the town, creating the valley that it was named for.

"There are excellent springs and streams all through the valley," George said, waving his hand at the hills around them.

"Is that why they call it Spring Valley?" Alice asked.

Uncle George nodded. "You've never seen soil like this, James. It is the perfect place for a farm."

Father and Mother exchanged glances, and Almanzo could almost hear his father's voice in his head saying, "We shall see."

"We are so looking forward to meeting Martha," Mother said. "I can't imagine what the woman is like who got my little brother to settle down." She smoothed down George's hair affectionately.

Uncle George laughed—a little nervously, Almanzo thought. "Well, she's very strong-willed," he said. "Like you, Angeline. And her family were some of the first settlers in this valley. See the Baptist church over there? Her father, Cutler Thayer, founded it."

"A fine thing," Father said, "to be part of the building of a new church in a wild place." He tugged on his beard as if he were imagining just where he might put a Methodist church in Spring Valley.

Almanzo craned his neck to look around as

the wagon rolled through the town. The streets here were dusty, and he did not see anything like Malone's Square, where Independence Day was always celebrated. Wooden planks formed a sidewalk on either side of the street. In places there was a roof above the sidewalk made by the balconies of the buildings or awnings coming off the upper levels of the stores. Almanzo saw one large, solid building with an impressive facade that would not have been out of place in Buffalo. Uncle George explained that it was a hotel called the Commercial House.

There were also many buildings going up. Uncle George's letter had been right about that. The town was like a beehive, with men striding about busily or standing in doorways, smoking and conversing. They passed one site where men were moving large limestone blocks into place for a foundation.

"It's so . . . civilized," Almanzo said quietly to Alice.

"You sound disappointed," she teased.

He was not disappointed, exactly. But this

was not the rugged pioneer life he had been imagining, far away from schools and hotels and stores. He would have to go even farther west for that, he guessed.

Almanzo was especially interested in the horses. He saw a few tied up to posts along the street and others drawing buggies and wagons like Uncle George's. But none of them were so fine as Father's, or half as handsome as Starlight. He wished he could ride Starlight down this street and out onto the prairie. Perhaps the girl from the train would see him and be impressed. Starlight would certainly love to have so much open space to run in. Almanzo felt a twist of sadness in him that could not be chased away even by the excitement of arriving at last.

"What's that?" Alice asked, pointing at a long, two-story brick building that sat up on a hill overlooking the town. The sunlight reflected cheerfully off its bright white roof and gleamed on the bell in the bell tower on top. The red bricks and sparkling windows along the sides looked new, and the white casements looked freshly painted.

"That is the schoolhouse," Uncle George said. "It has eight rooms and ten fine teachers. The townsfolk are very proud of it."

"Oh, that is wonderful," Mother said happily. "Almanzo need not miss any schooling after all. He and Alice can attend classes while we are here."

"Lucky Almanzo," Father said with a smile.

Almanzo's heart sank. Suddenly the building did not look so cheerful or friendly anymore. It looked more like the Academy than the one-room schoolhouse he was used to. It looked *very* civilized. He did not want to be trapped indoors with books and slates. He wanted to be out exploring this new land and finding them a good place to live.

But Father was nodding, and Alice looked pleased. He knew he could not argue, so he said nothing. But he thought to himself that Perley was very fortunate he did not have to go to school for a long time yet.

The dust from the road rose up and stuck in Almanzo's nose and throat as they rode in Uncle George's wagon. Uncle George explained that many of the townspeople were farmers who lived outside the town, farming their land. His own land was at the north end of town, and he was mighty proud of it. He talked about the rich soil and his crops all the way home. Almanzo thought there was a nervous way about Uncle George, as if he talked about farming so he would not have to talk about something else.

When they pulled up to Uncle George's house, Almanzo was surprised to see how small it was. It did not seem large enough for them all to fit in standing up, let alone sleep in. A woman came to the door, wiping her hands on her apron, as they pulled up. Uncle George hopped down to help unload their trunks. Then he hurried off to the stable with the horses in his nervous, quick way. He did not say a word to his wife, who stood on the front steps staring at the Wilders.

"Good day to you, ma'am," Father said politely, taking off his hat. "I am James, and this is Angeline, and these are our children, Alice and Almanzo and little Perley."

"You must be Martha," Mother said, shifting Perley in her arms. "It is so nice to finally meet you, after all of George's warm letters about you."

Aunt Martha did not look like she thought it was nice to meet them. She was much younger than Mother, with green eyes that might have been pretty if they hadn't looked so tired, but her face was severe and very grim, and her sandy brown hair was pulled back tightly, rolled under, and pinned at the base of her neck. Her eyes fixed on Perley as if he were a stray dog that might sneak into her house and break everything. She did not return his friendly, gap-toothed smile.

"You brought your children," she said with a sigh.

"Of course," said Father. "We said we would in our letter. Surely you received it?"

"We thought these three were too young to be left behind," Mother explained. Almanzo could tell she was startled by Martha's discourtesy. Mother was always delighted when her brothers and sisters brought their children to visit. The more people there were in the house, the happier she was.

"Even with relatives?" Aunt Martha said, raising her eyebrows. Before they could answer, she went on, "Well, never mind. It is too late now. I suppose you should come in."

Mother and Father exchanged a look. "I'd better go see if George needs help in the stable," Father said. Almanzo wished he could go with him. Walking into the house under Aunt Martha's stern gaze made him feel like a caterpillar crawling past a crow's fierce, sharp beak. Alice looked worried, too. Almanzo took her hand and squeezed it, and she gave him a small smile.

The house was not much better on the inside than it was on the outside. There were only three rooms downstairs and a small attic upstairs. One room was the kitchen, where red gingham curtains were drawn tightly over the windows. Tiny slivers of sunshine snuck around the edges, but most of the room was aglow in a dusky red light. Crumbs were scattered across the kitchen table and all around the wood-burning stove on the far wall. In the corner, a wet rag was tossed carelessly over the edge of a bucket full of soapy water.

Almanzo could see his mother's face tighten. Her fingers twitched on Perley's back. He knew she wanted to take a broom and give the place a good brisk cleaning. Their home in New York would never be left in such a state, especially with guests expected.

Aunt Martha led them into the sitting room, where two rocking chairs were set by an iron stove. A pallet filled with straw was lying in one corner, with two pillows and a set of sheets folded on top of it. A carpet made of red and white and blue rags woven together was on the floor, and a low footstool sat by the stove. On the walls were two embroidered samplers with quotes from the Bible. That was all that was in the room.

Aunt Martha did not show them the third room, but Almanzo guessed that was the bedroom where she and Uncle George slept.

Almanzo thought of their big, warm house in Malone, with its shelves of books and the tall elegant clock and cozy chairs and pretty wallpaper. He had not expected to miss home so soon. He wondered if he could ever feel comfortable in a house like this.

Had he made the wrong choice in coming here? He could be at home happily riding Starlight or eating pancakes with Royal right now, instead of worrying about where he would sleep and whether Aunt Martha disliked him already.

He stood by the door as Aunt Martha went in and sat in one of the rocking chairs. Mother paused a moment, and then sat down in the other one with Perley in her lap. The baby had slept in the wagon, and now he leaned against her shoulder, his cheeks flushed pink and his sweet blue eyes drooping sleepily. Almanzo did not understand why Aunt Martha seemed so displeased to see him. Perley was a good baby. Perhaps she just needed to know him better.

Alice sat on the footstool and Almanzo went to stand beside her. Although it was warm outside, there was a chill in the room. The wooden floorboards seemed bare and cold under Almanzo's boots. They all sat for a moment in silence. Almanzo could see that Mother was about to speak, but then Father and Uncle George came in stamping their feet. Father was asking Uncle George about his crops, but he looked at Mother as they came in, and it seemed to Almanzo that they were having the same thought, although he did not know what it was.

"Well," Aunt Martha said, interrupting her husband as he answered Father. "I don't know where all of these people are to sleep, but they're your family, so I'm sure you can work something out, George. I'll go see if we have enough food for everyone for supper." She got up, brushing down her skirts.

"I will help you," Mother said in a voice that was not to be argued with. She handed Perley over to Alice, and he cuddled into her arms as the two women left the room. When no one else was looking, Almanzo blew up his cheeks and made a funny face at the baby, and Perley giggled.

Uncle George rubbed his chin, looking anxious. "Perhaps we could set up more pallets in the attic for your older two," he said in his raspy voice. "But I don't know where the baby should sleep."

"Almanzo and I can make a crib for Perley," Father said. "Almanzo is an excellent woodworker." Almanzo felt a glow of pride. He stood up taller and straightened his shoulders. Perhaps he could be useful, and then maybe Aunt Martha would be glad they were there.

"All right," Uncle George said slowly. "There are not many trees here yet, but I'm sure we can spare some lumber."

"Why don't we take a walk?" Father said. "I've been looking forward to seeing this fine farm of yours."

Uncle George's face brightened, and he nodded. Father looked over to Almanzo and Alice. "Come along, you two," he said. "You should see where we'll be working, if we're to be a help and not a burden."

They all saw the look of doubt on Uncle George's face. Father said, "These two have been helping on my farm for years. Alice is like a little cart horse—strong and determined. And Almanzo is a hard worker who has a fine, deft hand with animals. I hope you'll give them a chance."

Uncle George only shrugged. Almanzo and Alice exchanged pleased looks over Perley's head. Hearing Father say that made Almanzo feel much better. He would work very hard to prove Father right, and he knew Alice would, too.

But he still couldn't help but wonder whether coming here was a mistake. Uncle George and Aunt Martha were not like their warm, friendly relatives back in New York. Their life seemed a lot harder and smaller than Almanzo had expected.

Was Spring Valley the right place for Almanzo's family?

Would it ever feel like home?

THE RUNAWAY

Living with Uncle George and Aunt Martha made everyone very anxious. Almanzo felt like he might do something wrong at any moment. He tried to stay as still as possible when he was in the house. He only spoke when he was spoken to. He helped with the chores as much as he could. He thought to himself that it was most unpleasant to live where you were not wanted.

Almanzo never imagined he would be so relieved to go to school. But as he and Alice walked through the long green grass to the road, he felt almost as if they were escaping from a prison, like in one of the novels that Eliza Jane sometimes read.

The misty morning air was alive with the hum of insects and bright bursts of birdsong. The sun was slowly peeking over the horizon, burning away the thin layer of clouds and turning the sky from gray to peach to pink, and then suddenly to brilliant, clear blue.

Almanzo took a deep breath of fresh air. He was glad to be away from the stuffiness of Uncle George's house. The attic where he and Alice slept was oppressively hot already, and summer had not yet come. He dreaded to think what it would be like in July.

But perhaps they would not still be there by then. Perhaps Mother and Father would decide they should all go home to Malone. He had heard them talking in low voices whenever they caught a moment away from George and Martha. Mother did not like being in someone else's house when they did not appear to be welcome, even though they had been invited. She missed Andrew and Sarah and her friends in Malone. Father was worried at the state of George's farm. Although the soil was as good as he'd said, George had been trying to do everything himself, and the farm had suffered. He needed sons like Royal and Almanzo to help with the crops and horses and livestock.

Almanzo had heard Mother say that must be why Martha was so tired—because she had been doing all the housework and trying to help George with the farm as well. Privately, Almanzo thought Mother could have done all that and more without ever even needing to sit down. And she would never let tiredness stop her from being generous and kind to her guests.

But he was sure that he and Father would be a help around the farm. Then perhaps everything would get better. He wasn't ready to leave Spring Valley yet. He hadn't had a chance to explore the town at all. He missed Royal, but he hoped he would meet other boys his own age at school. And at least he had Alice for company.

Together they climbed the hill to the big brick schoolhouse. As they came closer, Almanzo saw a group of boys racing around the yard. Some of them looked to be his age, and some of them seemed younger. One small boy, who was perhaps eight or nine years old, was yelling out instructions to the others as he ran.

They were so intent on their game that they did not notice Alice and Almanzo. It was the girls gathered around the steps of the school-house who spotted them first. Almanzo could see them lean in to whisper to one another. Alice stepped a little closer to him.

"Don't be afraid," he said. "Or if you are, don't let anyone see it."

"I'm not afraid," she said, tossing her curls. "They're just girls. It's no different from the Academy."

Almanzo knew that Alice had been nervous about going to the Academy at first, too. But she was good at acting brave.

"Hi, look out there!" a voice yelled behind them. "Look out!"

Almanzo heard the beating of hooves on the road. He turned and saw a large black horse thundering down on them. Its sides were heaving, flecked with white foam, and its eyes rolled with terror. Its reins were flapping long and loose around its legs. Almanzo felt a bolt of fear for the horse—what if the reins got tangled in its hooves? That could bring the horse crashing to the ground, badly injured.

"Whoa!" he called, stepping forward. "Shhh, steady!"

"Manzo, careful!" Alice cried.

The horse was moving too fast. It probably hadn't even spotted Almanzo yet, and it was almost on top of him. Without thinking twice, Almanzo stepped to the side and seized the loose reins as the horse galloped past. The horse jerked its head back, rearing in place. It turned toward Almanzo, but he had already grabbed the saddle and flung himself onto the horse's back.

"Shhhh," he murmured, letting the horse continue its turn into a wide circle. He held the reins firmly in both hands, sitting into the saddle and keeping his legs loose instead of braced. "Whoa there, handsome." The horse snorted and jumped, tossing its head to try and break free, but as it realized that Almanzo was in control, it calmed down. Its gallop slowed to a trot, and soon Almanzo was able to bring it around to a stop. The horse's head drooped, and Almanzo could feel it heaving deep breaths underneath him.

"There's a good fellow," Almanzo said, patting the horse's neck. His hand came away slick with the horse's sweat, and he realized that he had probably dirtied his good school clothes . . . and he hadn't even gotten to school yet! Mother would not be pleased with him.

"More of a lady than a fellow," said a boy's voice. "Although she's not being very ladylike right now. Are you, Velvet?" Almanzo looked down and saw the boy from the train station. He looked flushed and out of breath, but his grin spread from one ear to the other. He must have been the one who'd called out to warn them about the runaway horse.

"Is she yours?" Almanzo asked.

"Afraid so," the boy said. "I don't know what got into her all of a sudden. She just bolted. Tipped me right into the dirt! That was amazing, how you stopped her. Thank you."

"Amazing?" Alice interjected, coming up behind him. "I'd call it foolhardy and reckless. Manzo, are you crazy? That horse could have run you over!"

"But did you see what he did?" the boy said. He was taller and older than Almanzo, but his face was lit up like he had just met a real cowboy. "I've never seen anyone our age ride like that."

Almanzo could feel his face turning red. "Aw, it wasn't anything," he said.

"And you!" Alice cried at the strange boy. "Letting your mad horse run wild! What if she had run all the way to the schoolyard and trampled one of the small children?"

"She wouldn't!" the boy said, bristling. "Velvet's a good horse! She's never run away on me before, and I ride her to the schoolhouse every day. Something must have spooked her, but I don't know what."

"Perhaps it was a bee sting," Almanzo said. He ran his hand along Velvet's neck and felt that her breathing had evened out and her trembling had stopped. Holding onto the reins, he swung himself down to the ground and led her over to the boy. "I saw that happen to one of my father's horses once. The quietest horse you ever saw, and all at once he was running like his tail was on fire."

"That could be it," the boy said, taking Velvet's reins. "I'd never have thought of that." He stroked her nose and murmured soothing sounds at her. Almanzo was glad to see that he handled her well. He'd wondered if the horse had been frightened by something the rider did wrong, but the boy looked like he knew what he was doing around a horse.

Alice's expression softened. Perhaps she was

also pleased to see that the boy did care about his horse. "A bee sting?" she said. "Poor horse. That would upset me, too."

"Enough to make you go galloping wild across the fields?" Almanzo teased.

"That would be funny," the boy said with a friendly grin.

Alice lifted her chin. "That would *not* be funny!" she said. "And you two are going to make me late for school." She turned and flounced away.

A group of girls was standing at the edge of the schoolyard, watching the whole scene. Almanzo saw two of them reach out for Alice and draw her in until she disappeared behind skirts and ringlets and ribbons. He could hear them saying, "You poor dear! That was terrifying! You could have been run over! Were you very frightened?"

He knew Alice hadn't been scared. She was too used to horses to be frightened of them. He didn't think she was really mad about his teasing, either. But he was glad to see that it had made the other girls be so friendly to her so quickly.

"Whew," said the boy. He clucked to Velvet and began leading her up to the schoolyard. Almanzo fell into step beside him. "That was an exciting start to the day," the boy said. "Welcome to Spring Valley, huh? You're new here, right? Didn't I see you getting off the train last week?"

"That's right," Almanzo said. "My name's Almanzo Wilder, but you can call me Manzo—everyone else does."

"I'm Albert Baldwin," said the boy. "Bert to my friends. And since you just saved my horse, I reckon you count as a friend." He shook Almanzo's hand. Almanzo felt warm and proud. Alice wasn't the only one making friends quickly. Perhaps school wouldn't be so bad after all.

FIRST DAY OF SCHOOL

Bert led Velvet to a hitching post behind the school, leaving Almanzo alone on the front steps. He wanted to follow and help with the horse, but the bell in the tower was already ringing, and he was afraid to be late on his first day. He ducked his head, took off his cap, and followed a group of six loud boys through the propped-open front door.

Inside the door was a long hallway, stretching to the back door of the schoolhouse. At either end of the hall there was a staircase up to the second floor and one down to the basement, where the furnace was. Four doors went off the hall into the schoolrooms. Almanzo could see clean, blank chalkboards and rows of desks through each door.

Students were moving quickly around the hall and in the rooms, choosing seats and talking to one another and laughing. It was busy and crowded and much bigger than the little schoolhouse he'd been going to since he was nine years old. It was almost as if they hadn't left Malone at all, and he thought it was quite unfair that he had come all this way to escape the Academy, only to end up in another school just like it.

Everyone seemed to know where they were supposed to go. Everyone except Almanzo. He stopped inside the door and looked around for Alice. She had attended the Academy for five years. Maybe she would know what to do here. The hall was full of skirts swaying and sunbonnets coming off and ribbons fluttering, but his sister was nowhere to be seen.

Almanzo caught a glimpse of a pale green cape with black velvet embroidery. The girl from the train station! He stood on his toes and craned his neck, trying to see over all the bonnets in his way.

"Hi, what are you, soft in the head?" Someone shoved him from behind and Almanzo stumbled forward, nearly falling on the wooden floor. A few of the nearest girls turned to see what the noise was about, but no one came to help him.

Almanzo turned, crushing his cap in his fist. His face felt warm with embarrassment and anger.

He was surprised to see that the boy who had pushed him was not even as tall as he was. He had red hair that was long around his ears and his clothes were all starched and pressed to look sharp and neat. He did not look like someone who got in fights. He did not look anything like Bill Ritchie and the other big Hardscrabble boys back in Malone, but his face was as mean as a wolverine's.

"Standing in the doorway gawping like the village idiot," the boy sneered. "I guess you belong in there." He flicked one hand at the closest classroom on the left. Almanzo could see that it was full of the littlest boys and girls, seven and eight years old. The ones who were sitting were squirming in their seats, and the others were pushing one another to get the desks in the back.

Almanzo didn't know what to say. Why would anyone be so uncivil to a total stranger?

"That's the first class," the strange boy said slowly and loudly. "For dirty farmer boys who don't know their alphabet yet."

Almanzo could feel himself turning red. "I know my alphabet," he said.

"Oh, it *can* talk," the boy said. Another boy standing behind him sniggered. This one was much bigger, with arms as wide around as Christmas hams. His nose was flat, like it had been mashed into his face.

"Shut up, Eddie," Bert said, coming through the front door and stamping his feet on the bristly horsehair mat. "Don't mind them, Manzo. Eddie's too scrawny to fight for himself and Elmer's too vacuously obtuse to figure out what I just said about him."

He took Almanzo's elbow and steered him briskly up the stairs before the bullies could respond. Almanzo glanced back as they went around the bend in the stairs. The redheaded boy was frowning angrily, and the big, flat-nosed boy had his mouth open, like a befuddled trout.

"What *did* you just say about him?" Almanzo asked.

"I called him dumb," Bert said with a grin. "Seems fair, doesn't it?" He led Almanzo into the bright upper hallway. Sunlight streamed through the tall windows in the classrooms. There were four rooms up here as well, with three big windows in each one: two along the side and one at the back.

"Eddie and Elmer are brothers," Bert said. "Twins, actually. Isn't that funny?"

"They don't look anything alike," Almanzo said, amazed.

"They're not," Bert said. "But Elmer follows Eddie around and does anything he says. He can be kind of a brute. Stay out of their way if you can."

"Well, we're off to a great start," Almanzo said, and Bert laughed.

"At least they're not in our class," Bert said. "Eddie probably could be, but they keep him back with Elmer." Almanzo wondered how Eddie felt about that.

He followed Bert into the second classroom on the right, feeling anxious. Was this the right place for him to be? The other boys and girls in the room all looked about Almanzo's age, fourteen or fifteen years old. But Bert seemed very smart. What if they were all that smart? What if they found out that Almanzo wasn't? Would Almanzo be sent back to the lower class with Eddie and Elmer?

A nice-looking man with a thick brown mustache stood at the front of the classroom, behind a long, wide desk. Almanzo thought he looked pleased to see Bert. He nodded to them in a friendly way and turned to the blackboard with a piece of chalk.

"Blast, the best seats are taken," Bert whispered, nodding to the last row of desks, right in front of the back window. Girls sat on one side and boys sat on the other, just the same as in Almanzo's little schoolhouse back in New York, but that was the only thing that was the same. Here the desks were all the right size for bigger students. Everyone in the room was studying the same subjects at once. They did not have to cram into desks that were too small. They did not have to read quietly while little girls recited their spelling, or try to answer history questions while little boys kicked and whispered. When the teacher rapped his ruler on the desk, the room became perfectly still.

Finally Almanzo saw Alice. She was sitting near the front of the room with a girl in a pretty blue dress. They were both looking at a map of the United States that was hanging on the wall beside the door.

Now Almanzo was really nervous. He was sure he should not be in the same class as Alice. She knew a lot more than he did, from studying at the Academy. But he didn't want to tell Bert that. He didn't want to leave the class and have to find where he was supposed to be by himself.

Almanzo and Bert chose a desk three rows from the front and sat together on the bench behind it. Almanzo felt very lucky that he had found a friend already. He would have been uncomfortable sitting by himself or with a stranger.

The teacher had written his name on the chalkboard: Mr. Lloyd. An American flag was pinned to the wall above the chalkboard. Almanzo had learned about the thirteen red and white stripes that stood for the original thirteen colonies. He knew that this flag had thirty-seven stars, one for each state in the union. It used to be thirty-six, but a new one had been added in 1867, when Almanzo was ten. That was when Nebraska became a state. Minnesota had not been a state for long, either—not even fifteen years yet.

Mr. Lloyd smiled at the class. "Welcome to school," he said. "Before we meet our new faces and begin assessing class levels, let's all rise to sing our anthem."

All the boys and girls stood up. Almanzo looked around nervously as he got to his feet. His school in New York never had singing, and there was no official American anthem. He did not know which song they were about to sing. Would it be "The Star-Spangled Banner"? Or "Yankee Doodle"?

Mr. Lloyd turned toward the flag and his low, deep voice started the song. Almanzo relaxed. It was "Hail, Columbia!," a patriotic song he had heard many times, especially during Independence Day parades. He lifted his chin and sang the chorus proudly with everyone else:

"Firm, united let us be,
Rallying round our liberty,

As a band of brothers joined,
Peace and safety we shall find."

The song always made Almanzo think of soldiers and war heroes. But Father said that it was farmers just as much as soldiers who had made America great.

Outside the tall glass windows, the sun shone brightly. Because the schoolhouse was on a hill, and the classroom was on the second floor, it seemed as if Almanzo could see for miles. The few bustling streets of Spring Valley were spread out below him. He could almost see all the way to his uncle's farm. He could see puffs of dust kicked up by the horses and wagons going along the main roads. He could see the tall grain elevators standing beside the railroad. Far in the distance, a thread of dark gray smoke showed that a train was on its way.

When they finished the song, Mr. Lloyd stepped to a low table beside his desk. On top of the table was a globe of the Earth, with all the countries of the world marked on it. Mr. Lloyd spun the globe with his long, slender fingers. "We'll start with Geography," he said.

Almanzo thought he heard a muffled groan from one of the boys behind him, but when Mr. Lloyd looked up sharply, the sound stopped right away.

"Since we have a number of new pupils this semester, this is just to see what you know and what you still need to learn. I will call you up two at a time. I'll ask you to point to a country on the globe. Then I'll ask you some questions about it, and we shall see what happens." Mr. Lloyd beckoned to the two girls nearest the wall in the front row, and they stood up, looking nervous. "In the meanwhile, the rest of you may take out your spellers and prepare for the next test."

There was a rustle of noise as all the students lifted the tops of their desks. A short stack of books was tucked inside each one. Almanzo ducked his head behind the desktop and whispered to Bert, "Tests already? On the first day?"

"Don't worry. Mr. Lloyd is swell," Bert whispered back. "He'll be fair about where he puts you."

That was exactly what Almanzo was worried about. It had been several months since he'd been to school. His family had been so busy preparing for the trip out to Spring Valley that he had not gone to the Academy, and he'd missed some of the winter term at the little schoolhouse. He was afraid that Eddie might be right, and that he did belong downstairs with the youngest children.

The long, complicated words in the speller made Almanzo's heart beat fast. He tried to concentrate on memorizing them, but he kept hearing questions from the front of the room like "How long is the Nile River?" and "In what year was the Siege of Belgrade?" He didn't know any of those things!

Then he heard Mr. Lloyd say, "Very good, Miss Wilder. It is unusual for a new student to get every question right."

Almanzo looked up and saw Alice smiling

her brightest smile. She waved to Almanzo as she went back to her seat. He saw her gaze move to Bert and he realized that his seatmate was watching her, too. Almanzo looked over in time to see Bert wink at her. Alice tossed her curls and sat down.

Too soon, Mr. Lloyd was calling Bert and Almanzo to the front of the room.

"Mr. Baldwin," the teacher said as they lined up before him. "I'm afraid two years is probably long enough for you in my classroom. We may not have the pleasure of your company anymore."

"Perhaps I forgot everything over the winter break," Bert said innocently.

"I doubt your father would allow that," Mr. Lloyd said with a smile.

"This is Almanzo Wilder," Bert said to the teacher.

"Miss Wilder's brother, I understand," Mr. Lloyd said.

"But I'm sure not as smart as her," Almanzo blurted out.

"Never fear, Mr. Wilder," said the teacher.

"Being smart is not necessarily the same as being educated, although it helps." Almanzo had no idea what Mr. Lloyd meant by that, but his expression was kind, and that made Almanzo feel better.

The globe hung from a steel wire holder. On the metal base were stamped the words "A. H. Andrews & Co." Mr. Lloyd started them off with easy questions, like finding Australia on the globe and "Who founded Quebec in Canada?" Then he asked them to point to certain rivers in Europe and cities in Asia. He asked about the history of India and the rebellion there. He asked about explorers from the sixteenth century. This was both Geography and World History. It made Almanzo's head spin. Mr. Lloyd's questions became more and more difficult. Almanzo got several of them wrong, but Bert answered every one.

"All right," Mr. Lloyd finally said. "Thank you, boys. You may sit down."

When all of the class had finished answering his questions, Mr. Lloyd picked up a speller from his desk.

"Let's try something different," he said. "Let's have a spelling bee."

Bert rubbed his hands together with a look of glee, but Almanzo's heart sank. Now the rest of the class would see how ignorant he was, too. He was starting to wish he had studied on the train, like Mother had wanted him to.

Mr. Lloyd lined them all up along the blackboard. He sat on a desk in the front row and read off the first word, "phenomenon." Almanzo was surprised when the first boy in the line got it wrong. Perhaps he was nervous, like Almanzo was. That made Almanzo *more* nervous.

The boy sat down, and Mr. Lloyd kept going down the line. The first girl spelled "emancipation" right, but the second girl went out on "nuisance." Five students in a row got words like "millionaire" and "surrender" right. Then came Alice, who got the word "rendezvous." It sounded like a different language to Almanzo, and he couldn't believe how she spelled it, but of course she was right.

Eventually Mr. Lloyd came to Almanzo. He ran his finger down the words in the speller and said, "Your word is 'commendable.'"

Almanzo took a deep breath. "C-o-m-m-e-n-d—" He paused. Was it "ible" or "able"? His palms felt damp, and he pressed his hands together, trying to remember. He'd have to guess. "A-b-l-e."

"Excellent," said Mr. Lloyd, and Almanzo breathed a sigh of relief. He had lasted through the first round.

Of the twenty-three students, six of them were out by the time Mr. Lloyd got to the end of the line. Five more went out in the next round, but Almanzo miraculously got "farrier"—a man who shoes horses—and he knew how to spell that. He even made it through "stomach" in the third round, when four other students sat down, but that was only because he had just seen it in the book and thought that the *h* at the end looked very odd.

Eight were left at the front of the room, including Alice, Almanzo, and Bert. Alice kept her chin up and didn't look over at them, but Bert kept stealing glances at her. Almanzo got the feeling that Bert wanted her to notice how clever he was.

"Mr. Wilder," said the teacher. "Your word is 'symptom.'"

"S-i-m-p-t-o-m?" Almanzo said, thinking hard.

"I'm afraid not," Mr. Lloyd said. "The second letter should be a *y*. But good work."

Almanzo sat down at his desk. He didn't mind. He was relieved he had lasted as long as he did. He was especially proud that Alice was still at the front of the room.

After seven rounds, only Alice and Bert were left. Now she did look at Bert, and Almanzo saw a twinkle in her blue eyes. He had forgotten how much she liked to compete.

Mr. Lloyd threw word after word at Alice and Bert, but neither one made a single mistake, no matter how hard the words were. Finally the teacher set down the speller and smoothed his hair with a laugh.

"I think it's clear that you both are a level beyond this class. I'll speak to Miss Thayer during lunch about moving you two up to the next class with her. Everyone else can stay with me." He went behind his desk and wrote something on a sheet of paper in neat, slanted handwriting.

Almanzo breathed a thankful sigh. He was not being sent down to a lower class. He could stay here with the other boys his age.

"Good match," Bert said to Alice, offering his hand. Her cheeks were pink as she shook it.

"I would have beaten you eventually," she said.

"Nobody beats me," Bert said with a friendly shrug.

"Nobody until me," she said, and went back to her seat. Bert sat down next to Almanzo, grinning.

"Sorry I won't be in this class with you," Bert said. "But I'll see you in the schoolyard at recess and midday."

"And maybe once I have a horse we can go

riding sometime," Almanzo said. It popped out before he knew what he was saying. Almanzo had no idea how long they would be staying, or if Father would want to buy any new horses here. But he missed Starlight with a powerful ache in his chest.

Riding Velvet, even for a short time, had reminded him of his horse back home and how he used to ride almost every day. Uncle George let Almanzo brush and tend his horses, but they were slow farm horses, not Morgans. It was nothing like having a beautiful horse that he had trained himself.

Even if the school was big and difficult, and even if Aunt Martha didn't like them, Almanzo thought he could imagine living here. But it couldn't be a real home until they had horses of their own, and it couldn't *really* feel like home until he was brushing down Starlight in the stall next to Royal and Flame.

He looked over at the big map of the states and found New York. It didn't look that far away from Minnesota. The corners of the map curled up like Alice's hair, and some of the names were faded in the sunshine. He could barely see the little dot that was Malone.

He wondered if Starlight missed him, too.

NOON AT LAST

The classroom was still and quiet. Everyone was reading. The only sound was the soft rustle of pages turning.

Cheerful sunlight poured in and turned the wooden floor a golden color. A light breeze blew through the open windows, smelling of sun and grass and fields and sky.

At noon Bert would go to a new classroom. For now he was still sitting next to Almanzo, sharing his reader. Almanzo could tell that Bert finished each page long before Almanzo did. But he sat patiently waiting for Almanzo to turn to the next page. Almanzo guessed he was reading each page twice while he waited.

Almanzo's long sleeves itched, and the button at the neck of his shirt felt tight. His shoes felt heavy on his feet. The words blurred on the page in front of him. It was only the first day of school, and he already wanted nothing more than to jump out the window and run free into the fields.

Also, he was very hungry. He had tried to eat a big breakfast, but it seemed like centuries had passed since that morning when, under Aunt Martha's disapproving eye, he had filled his plate with thick slabs of juicy bacon, fresh bread with yellow butter melting on it, piles of scrambled eggs. . . .

Rrrrrowl, went his stomach. *Rrrrrwwrrr.*

Bert pressed his hand to his mouth. Almanzo could see that he was trying not to laugh. Mr. Lloyd looked up, his mustache crinkling as he tried to figure out what the disturbance was. But Almanzo's stomach was mercifully quiet again. He tried not to think about food. He wondered what was in the dinner pail under Alice's desk. He wondered how long it was until noon.

Finally Mr. Lloyd set down the last slate he'd been reviewing. He pulled out his pocket watch. All the students sat forward hopefully. He tucked it away again and linked his hands together.

"It is noon," he said. "You may go outside for lunch or eat in here, if you wish. In one hour we will meet Miss Lowe downstairs for music lessons with the other upper classes."

Music lessons! Almanzo had never had any such thing.

Most of the boys grabbed their dinner pails and bolted for the door. Several of the girls pulled out checkered napkins and spread them over their desks, including the girl in the blue dress beside Alice. Almanzo went over to his sister with Bert right behind him.

"Can we eat outside?" he pleaded. "Look how nice the weather is."

"Oh, no!" said the girl beside Alice. "You mustn't, Alice, you'll spoil your lovely complexion."

Alice hesitated. She twisted one curl of brown hair around her finger, looking out at the sunny green day. She looked back at Almanzo's anxious face. He didn't think he could bear it if he had to spend another minute inside the classroom walls.

"All right," she relented. "I'll stay out of the sun and keep my bonnet up," she reassured her seatmate as she got to her feet. Almanzo felt sure that he had the best sister in the world. Alice more than made up for the bossiness of Eliza Jane. She was a good friend to have in a strange new place, especially if he couldn't have Royal. He grinned happily as they clattered down the stairs to the schoolyard with Bert.

Alice found a bench in the shade around the side of the school and began to unpack their dinner pail while Almanzo went with Bert to check on Velvet. The horse was on a tether long enough for her to reach the ground, and she was munching a mouthful of grass as they came up to her. Thin green stems stuck out of the corners between her teeth. Her eyes were soft and brown. She seemed nothing like the wild horse that had galloped along the road that morning, except that Almanzo could see the strength in her long legs and sturdy back. He stroked her neck while Bert murmured to her and gave her carrots from his pockets.

Alice made Almanzo wash his hands at the pump behind the schoolhouse before he could eat. The dinner pail was full of wonderful food, most of it made by Mother while Aunt Martha fretted about how much children ate. There were chunks of hard cheese with a sharp, salty flavor; hearty, nutty-tasting slices of graham bread with sweet blackberry preserves; thick sausages; and fluffy doughnuts that Almanzo had watched Mother fry the night before.

Eating outside was a treat, with the wind ruffling Almanzo's hair and the sun warming him from tip to toe. He watched the other boys run around the yard playing Cowboys and Indians. The small boy he'd noticed that morning was in charge again, telling the other boys which side they were on and leading the Indians off to hide around the other side of the schoolhouse.

"Who is that?" Almanzo asked Bert, nodding at the younger boy.

"That's Dick Sears," Bert said. "His father owns a wagon shop downtown, on Vine Avenue. He's a smart little kid. Hey, Richard!"

The boy veered away from the other boys and came running over. He bounced from foot to foot as if he couldn't stand still.

"Dick, this is Almanzo," Bert said. "Tell him what you told me at the end of winter term."

"About what?" the boy said with wide eyes.

"About how you're going to own your own watch store one day," Bert said.

"Oh, sure," Dick said. "I'm going to name it after myself and everyone will want my watches and they'll be the best ever and lots of people will work for me and I'm going to be famous and—" His gaze fell on something behind them. "Uh-oh," he said. He turned and ran back to the other boys.

"So remember the name Sears," Bert said with a grin. Almanzo twisted around to see what had scared Dick away.

The twins, Eddie and Elmer, were coming down the steps of the schoolhouse. Eddie had his face twisted in a scowl, and Elmer was cracking his knuckles. This might have worried Almanzo, but his attention was distracted. Because leaning against the side of the steps was a group of girls, and in the middle of them was the girl from the train station.

She was even prettier than he'd remembered. He thought she might be about thirteen years old, a year younger than he was. Her brown hair looked like it curled naturally, with small tendrils framing her heart-shaped face under a pink and white sunbonnet. Her dress was also pink, and it seemed very fashionable to him, although he didn't know anything about girls' dresses. She was laughing at something one of the other girls had said.

"Manzo, you pack away the dinner things," Alice said, getting up and shaking the crumbs off her skirt. She hurried over to the girls and joined their conversation. Almanzo could hear them all giggling together. He wondered what girls talked about. It seemed like all they did was talk and talk, all the way through recess. They might as well be grown-ups already, sitting in their living rooms drinking tea and having long, boring conversations about the weather and roads and dress patterns.

A few of the other boys from his class came up, and Bert introduced them to Almanzo.

"Do you know how to play baseball?" asked a stocky boy named Joshua.

"No," said Almanzo, "but I have played other ball games, and I am a good catcher."

"Maybe you can play with us after school," said a boy with curly blond hair named Victor.

"I have to help with chores today," Almanzo said. "But perhaps tomorrow." He would ask Father for permission. All the boys nodded. They all had chores to do at home, too, whether their fathers were farmers or storekeepers or wagon makers or blacksmiths or doctors.

The belfry bell rang to signal the end of the dinner hour. Almanzo remembered that the next thing was music lessons. He stayed close to Bert and Joshua as they crowded up the front steps into the downstairs hallway. All the bigger students were going into the far classroom on the left. Already Almanzo could hear notes of music.

But he was still surprised when he saw the organ against the wall of the classroom. It was a proper organ, shinier and newer than the one in the church in Malone. Almanzo thought the people of Spring Valley must really care about school to spend so much money on this schoolhouse.

The organ's wood was a glowing, dark red-brown with a matching bench. The two wide foot pedals that kept air going into the pipes to make the organ sound were covered in big squares of light blue cloth. The keys were white like snow and black like Velvet's nose. Curving vine patterns were carved into the front and sides of the organ, and the stop knobs were a warm polished brass.

A woman with pale blond hair sat at the organ, touching the keys with her fingers. Almanzo remembered that Mr. Lloyd had said the music teacher's name was Miss Lowe. She was dumpy and stout, and her face looked like it had been put together wrong—nose too big, eyes too wide apart, mouth crooked, ears too small. She did not look up at them as they came into the room. Her eyes were fixed on the organ.

There were no seats in this classroom. All the boys lined up on one side of the room and all the girls on the other. Eddie and Elmer pushed and shoved their way to the back and then kicked anybody who got too close to them. Almanzo's heart thumped when he saw the pretty girl standing next to Alice. She had taken off her sunbonnet, and she kept touching her hair. Her smile lit up her face like a fire flaring to life. It was like candy on Christmas, thrilling even though you expected it, and even after you'd eaten as much of it as your stomach could take.

The students were still jostling and talking when the woman at the keyboard said, without turning around, "We'll start with scales." She began playing immediately. Most of the girls and a few boys were quick enough to jump in right away, but it took the rest of them several moments to catch up. Almanzo moved his mouth so no one would notice that he wasn't singing yet. He wasn't sure that he would be doing the right thing.

"La, la, la, la, la," the students sang, going up the scale. "La, la, la, la, la," going back down. That seemed easy enough. Almanzo joined in for the second round. The teacher kept going until everyone was standing still, singing instead of talking, even Eddie and Elmer. Then she started playing a hymn that Almanzo recognized from church. He relaxed a little more. This was fun—more fun than reading. And as long as he didn't stare, he could sometimes look over at the girl next to Alice, who seemed to be smiling even when she was singing.

The third song was "Yankee Doodle Dandy," which Almanzo loved to sing on Independence Day. It reminded him of marching in the parade around Malone's central square. Miss Lowe's fingers were strong and fast on the organ keys. She made beautiful sounds come out of it, and she smiled a little as she played. He could see his teacher, Mr. Lloyd, standing outside in the hall, listening.

After "Yankee Doodle," Miss Lowe finally turned around and began teaching them about notes and parts and keys. She drew lines on the blackboard and circles between the lines and on the lines. It all sounded confusing to Almanzo, but he tried to listen attentively, because her voice was soft and she seemed almost as nervous as he had been that morning. He was relieved when she went back to playing and let them sing some more.

Once he looked up and thought he caught the girl from the train station looking at him, but she looked away so quickly that he could have been wrong. He was tremendously surprised after class when she and Alice came up to him and Bert as everyone spilled into the hall. He had forgotten that Bert must know her, since he had seen them together at the train station.

"Albert, would you stop at the general store on the way home?" she said in a sweet voice. "Mother was hoping for some more pink thread so we could finish embroidering my handkerchiefs, and I need another slate pencil."

"We could go together," Bert suggested. "Velvet can carry two."

She gave a delicate shudder. "No, thank you. I prefer to walk." Almanzo guessed that she had seen the horse running wild that morning. He couldn't blame her for being wary of Velvet. She linked her arm in Alice's, and they started up the stairs together.

"That's my cousin Catherine," Bert said. Almanzo was glad he hadn't had to ask. "Her family is staying with us until they buy their own land out here." He didn't say anything else about her, and Almanzo thought it would seem odd if he asked any questions. At the top of the stairs, he saw Catherine disappear into the first classroom on the left. Mr. Lloyd was waiting to take Bert and Alice to the room beyond that one.

Almanzo went back to his desk by himself. Now he would not have to share his books, but he would have to sit alone. He lifted the top and looked inside, pretending to be busy with something. He didn't want to sit staring into space while everyone else came in.

He felt a nudge at his shoulder and turned around. Joshua was passing a slate forward to him. Almanzo took it and read the message on it: *Baseball tomorrow. Ask your pa! The sandlot after school. We have a bat for you.*

Almanzo passed it back with a grin, nodding. He was sure Father would let him play if he did all his chores well tonight. Soon he would have more friends. It would be just like Malone, only better, because they lived closer to town and he could see other boys more often. Maybe one of them would even have a horse he could ride sometimes.

It wouldn't be the same as having Starlight, but it still made him feel better. Outside Aunt Martha's house, Spring Valley wasn't too bad at all.

LETTERS FROM HOME

A storm was blowing around Uncle George's little house. Almanzo could hear the rain splattering across the roof like small horses galloping over the shingles. A roll of thunder went *boom boom boom* and lightning darted behind the closed shutters.

The orange candle flame was warm and comforting in the midst of such noise. Almanzo huddled closer to it, rolling his pen between the fingers of his right hand. His left hand rested on the pile of letters on the table.

The room was snug and dry. Father and Almanzo had gone around the house last Saturday, filling in the cracks and chinks and making sure the roof did not leak anywhere. Almanzo thought his aunt and uncle must have been very cold and wet over the winter, from all the holes they found. He hoped they would be happier about their guests once they saw how useful the Wilders could be.

Aunt Martha was rocking in her chair with her deep red woolen shawl wrapped around her. She looked nearly asleep. Mother sat in the other chair, singing a quiet lullaby to Perley. Father had gone out to the barn with Uncle George to check on the horses and cows.

Almanzo and Alice were both sitting at the table with pens and ink and paper. They were supposed to be writing to Royal and Eliza Jane, back home in Malone. Mother and Father had started the letter. There only space for a few lines at the end, and they must not waste the paper by leaving any of it empty. Almanzo wanted to ask about Starlight. But he could not think of anything else to say. It was odd, for he always had plenty to say to Royal when they were together. He wished they could go riding and talk instead of having to write letters like this.

He rested his foot on the crossbeam of his chair, feeling again a swell of pride that he had made the chair himself. Father had bought good tools and lumber with his own money, and after making a crib for Perley, together he and Almanzo had built a new table and new chairs for Uncle George and Aunt Martha. Uncle George had offered to pay for it, but Father said that it was a gift—and anyway, Alice and Almanzo needed it so they could have somewhere to study.

That was true. Almanzo would not have wanted to study on the floor in the hot, stuffy attic. It made him nervous to be downstairs with Aunt Martha watching him study, but at least he could breathe, and his penmanship was much neater at a table.

Alice drew Mother's letter closer to her and began to write at the bottom. Almanzo leaned over and saw that she was describing the schoolhouse. He knew they mustn't complain about Aunt Martha in these letters. It was not good manners, and they should be grateful that Uncle George was letting them stay with him. Even if Mother and Father agreed with Almanzo, they would be very displeased to hear him say anything about it.

He picked up the last letter from Eliza Jane and Royal. Most of the page was covered in Eliza Jane's feathery script, all the letters flowing together neatly as if she had bossed them into an orderly line like her students. At the bottom Royal had crammed two lines into the small space she had left, his handwriting dotted with ink spots and full of misspellings.

Dear Mother and Father and Alice and little Manzo, Eliza Jane had written. "Little Manzo"! He was nearly fifteen years old! And almost as tall as Royal! He shook his head.

I have decided that everyone must call me EJ instead of Eliza Jane from now on. You should start practicing for when you return. Royal never can seem to remember. It has been unseasonably cold here for June, which wears upon my nervous system, and I needed to take a week to recover after we planted all the corn, as it made me quite tired. But you need not worry about the farm. I have been managing the accounts and everything is quite satisfactory. The chickens are laying well, so we were able to sell a few eggs on Mother's account at the store in town, and all were pleased to see that the Wilder farm is still in production, thanks to my hard work (and Royal's). Aunt Sarah and Uncle Andrew send their love, and you are much missed at the church as well. I must say, I wonder where the new Sunday school teacher went to school; it cannot have been anywhere as refined as the Academy, for she has dreadful posture at the organ—

Almanzo yawned and skipped ahead. Eliza Jane went on and on about the details of town life and how the tomatoes were doing and which times of day she felt ill and how she had bought a new hat and what it looked like. Then toward the end she wrote:

I hope Manzo is applying himself to his studies. There is nothing more valuable than a good education! Manzo, write me a nice long letter and show me how your grammar and spelling have improved now that you are at a proper school. Tell us something that is not about horses. What is your teacher like? Do you go every day now? I hope Father isn't letting you get away with any laziness! These are the most important years for learning!

Almanzo snorted indignantly. She was hundreds of miles away, and she was *still* bossing him around! And he had never stayed home from school out of laziness—only to help Father on the farm, which was the very opposite of laziness.

Royal's lines at the bottom said only: *The farm is well. No land sales here lately—nobody* *wants farmland—only to build stores. That is where the $$ is. Manzo, S. is a very fine horse.* His name was an illegible scrawl in the last corner of space.

Almanzo turned the letter over, hoping again that he'd find another scrap of news from Royal that he'd missed before, but there was nothing but Eliza Jane's long ramblings. He set it down again, feeling dissatisfied. He *knew* Starlight was a very fine horse. Couldn't Royal give him any more useful news than that?

"There," Alice said, signing her name with a flourish. "Now you can end it. Don't worry, there's not much more space to fill."

She slid the letter over to Almanzo. He grinned when he saw she had written that Miss Thayer was "the finest teacher I've ever met." They both knew that would rile up Eliza Jane, who acted as if she was the best teacher in the whole country.

Alice glanced at Aunt Martha, who was making a soft buzzing noise now that meant she was fast asleep. "Did you see what Mother and Father wrote?" she whispered softly.

"Are we allowed to read it?" Almanzo asked.

"I don't see how we couldn't," Alice said. "It's mostly about how they miss Royal and Eliza Jane, along with questions about how real estate is doing out there and whether the hops crop has improved this year."

"Hmm," Almanzo said. That didn't sound very interesting at all.

"And," Alice said, lowering her voice even further, "they mention that the plot of land next door to Uncle George's is for sale."

Almanzo stared at the letter. That was much more exciting news. Was Father thinking of buying it? Then they could go home and get Starlight and move here for real.

"Okay," Alice said, dipping his pen in the ink for him. "Now you write something."

Almanzo bent over the paper, writing carefully in the flickering candlelight. He didn't want to give Eliza Jane anything to lecture him about in her next letter. The paper was smooth and cool under his ink-stained fingers. He wasn't sure how he had gotten ink all over his hands before even writing a word, but he was cautious not to smudge the letter.

Dear Royal and Liza Jane, he wrote. He knew she did not like that nickname—any more than he liked to be called "little Manzo"!

It is warm here. We had cold roast chicken sandwiches for lunch because it was too hot to eat anything else. The schoolhouse is very big. We picked plums along the fences and Mother made plum jam for breakfast. We ate it with warm biscuits. I guess it was not too warm for biscuits. Perley ate more plum jam than any of us and got it all over his face. Later we even found some behind his ears! He is getting pretty good at walking on his own now. I met a boy with a horse named Velvet. She is a pretty horse, but not as handsome as Starlight. She has soft black ears and a streak of white in her tail. Is Starlight eating well? Do you take him out riding every day? Have you driven him to town with the buggy? Does he still look

in your jacket for carrots when you go to the
stable? Can you hear him whinny at Flame in
the middle of the night?

He stopped, realizing that he had written mostly about horses even though Eliza Jane had said not to. She would be very stern about that. He thought for a moment, tapping the end of the pen against his nose. Finally he added, *Uncle George's barn has three stray cats living in it. They are good mousers. Has the barn cat had kittens again this year, and did you give them away?*

Then he crammed his initial into the bottom corner and pushed the paper back to Alice. She read over what he had written and laughed.

"Do you think Mother and Father won't approve?" he asked worriedly.

"It's fine," Alice said. "Besides, Royal will like it."

The candle flame danced and guttered in a sudden gust of wind, and they heard the door in the kitchen close behind Father and Uncle

George. Father was saying something, but he paused as Uncle George had a long coughing fit. Aunt Martha frowned a little in her sleep. Mother looked up with a concerned expression, and Perley sleepily patted her face as if he wanted her to keep singing.

Finally Uncle George recovered enough to say, "I think it's a fine idea, James. You know this land is good. You've seen how well my crops are doing."

"Angeline thinks it is too soon," Father said in a low voice. "We have not been here very long." Almanzo could hear them taking off their boots and washing their hands in the basin of water by the door. He exchanged a look with Alice. They were both sitting very still, hoping to hear something interesting.

"But I dislike imposing on you like this," Father went on. Almanzo thought that was a civil way of putting it. As far as he could tell, he and Father had done more work around the farm in the last month than Uncle George had been able to do in a year. What Father really meant, surely, was that he wanted to get out of their house and live somewhere where they wouldn't feel so unwanted.

Mother cleared her throat, politely, but loud enough to let Father know that they could all hear him. After a moment, he came into the room with Uncle George. Father went over to stoke the fire while Uncle George sat down heavily in one of the chairs at the table. His face was pale, and his breathing sounded like sandpaper over knotted wood.

Father put one hand on Mother's shoulder and patted Perley's small golden head.

"Time for bed," he said to Almanzo and Alice.

Almanzo stacked the letters neatly and screwed the top on the inkwell. Alice cleaned the pens. They said good night to Uncle George and Aunt Martha, who woke up a little bit as they went to the door of the sitting room.

"Sleep well. If the weather is better, we're going for a long walk tomorrow," Father said mysteriously. He gave Almanzo his twinkling look.

Alice and Almanzo hurried up the stairs to the attic. He changed into his nightclothes and got ready for bed with the sound of the rain dancing close above his head. The rain had cooled the attic a bit, but Almanzo did not care that it was hot, or that he was sleeping on a straw-filled mattress on the floor, or that the storm was even louder up here. He could guess where they were walking to tomorrow.

Their new home!

AN UNEXPECTED MEETING

The sun was shining brightly the next morning. The air smelled fresh and clean after the rainstorm. Drops of water sparkled on the leaves and the grass, which was damp and cool beneath Almanzo's bare feet. He wriggled his toes happily. It was nice to leave his boots behind on such a sunny, summery day.

Alice was barefoot too. Mother disapproved, but Father had said it was all right. They followed their parents through Uncle George's vegetable patch, feeling the rich dirt crumble between their toes. Father offered Mother his arm, and they walked slowly around the newly planted field of wheat, toward the stream that marked the edge of Uncle George's land.

They'd left Perley with Aunt Martha. Almanzo thought Martha liked Perley a little better now that she'd seen he wasn't the kind of baby who cried all the time. Once in a while he even caught her smiling at Perley's funny gurgles.

Blackbirds flapped overhead, dark against the bright blue sky. The low hum of insects murmured all around them, and Almanzo saw grasshoppers leaping in the bushes. Two squirrels chased each other across a patch of grass, around and around and finally up a tree. He could see their fluffy gray tails whisking between the branches as they played.

The stream up ahead was a ribbon of silver, winding through a stand of small trees. Almanzo whooped and ran on ahead, turning a somersault in the long grass that whisked against his legs and tickled his nose. Mother said "Almanzo!" but Father laughed. His eyes were bright, as if he wished he could be doing somersaults too.

Almanzo splashed into the water. It was cold and fierce against his bare feet. The river stones were polished smooth from being in the water so long. He felt the tickle of something brush his ankle. It was a fish! The stream was full of darting shadows and the silvery gleam of fish. They did not hide in the reeds when people came into the stream. They must not know about men with fishing rods. Father and Almanzo could catch many trout here, like they had back in New York whenever it rained.

"Oh dear, James," Mother said, stopping at the stream and lifting her skirts above her shoes. It was a small stream, but it was a little too wide to jump. She looked around for a stepping-stone to cross on.

"Don't you worry, Angeline," Father said. And then he scooped her up in his arms! Mother gasped and held on to his neck as he carried her across the stream. When he set her down on the other side, she brushed off her skirt and said, "James, really!" but her voice was teasing and Almanzo saw that she was smiling.

They were not on Uncle George's land anymore. A man had bought this land last year, but now he was going to sell it. Father wanted to speak to him and find out why—and how much he wanted for it.

They walked on through the trees and out into the fields, where patches of young wheat were growing in odd clumps instead of straight lines. Almanzo thought of Father's stories about lazy farming. It did not look as if this farmer had harrowed or planted properly.

A thick row of glossy, dark green hedges grew around the edges of the field. Suddenly Almanzo noticed that one of the bushes was shaking.

"Father, look," he said, pointing to it.

They all stopped and stared. The bush was making grunting and growling noises.

"It could be a wild animal," Father said. They all thought of wolves, which sometimes howled across the prairies. Or perhaps it was a bear, like the one Almanzo had seen once while berrying in New York. Or it could be a badger, or some other animal Almanzo had never encountered.

"Perhaps it belongs on this farm," Almanzo said. "Perhaps it's an escaped pig, or a calf, or a sheep."

Mother pulled Alice closer to her and backed away from the bush. Father lifted his walking stick, ready to protect them. The bush shook and growled and snorted, and then through the leaves Almanzo saw a curly black and white tail low to the ground. He relaxed. "It's a pig," he said. "Like Lucy. I'll go get it."

"Be careful, Mannie," Alice said.

Almanzo crept up to the bush. He crouched down near the ground. He yelled "Ha!" and leaped forward, tackling the back end of the pig.

The pig yelped wildly, lunged forward, slipped out of his arms, and then spun around and knocked Almanzo onto his back. It planted two paws on his shoulders and panted into his face with a goofy grin.

It wasn't a pig at all. It was a dog!

It was one of the strangest dogs Almanzo had ever seen. It was small, the same size as Lucy, the pig he had raised, and just as fat. Its tail was small and curly and only a bit longer than a pig's. It had short black fur with white patches. Its ears were wide and stuck up straight like two big triangles on top of its head. A long pink tongue lolled out of its mouth.

Almanzo saw Father coming with his walking stick raised. "It's all right!" he said. "He's only playing." He scratched the dog behind its big ears. Its whole back end shook as it tried to wag its little tail. Almanzo sat up, rolling the dog off him, and got to his feet. The dog stood up on its back legs and looked up at him with bright black eyes.

"You gave us such a fright, Almanzo," Mother scolded. "And look what a mess you've made of yourself." She whacked his jacket briskly, trying to shake loose some of the dirt.

"Perhaps he belongs to the farmer," Father said. "He'll run along home in a moment."

But the dog followed Almanzo all the way to the shanty house on the far side of the fields. It kept looking up at him like it wanted to play. Almanzo couldn't believe that such a fat little dog had so much energy. He liked the way it always seemed to have a silly grin on its face.

He wished he could keep it, but he knew Father would not approve. Father thought dogs should be useful—for herding sheep or protecting livestock from predators or scaring off thieves. This dog looked anything but useful.

A large man with a long blond beard was standing at the edge of the field outside the shanty, leaning on a hoe. He was staring at the ground like it had offended him. Only his jaw was moving, chewing a piece of tobacco. As they came closer, he squinted at Father. Suddenly Almanzo felt ashamed of his dirty jacket and bare feet. He hoped the farmer would not misjudge Father because of how Almanzo looked.

"Good morning," Father said. "I'm James Wilder. I understand you might be looking to sell this land."

The man spit on the ground. "That be so. My wife wants to go back east." Then he said a word Almanzo had never heard before, but he could tell that it was bad from the look on Father's face.

Mother put one hand on Almanzo's shoulder and one on Alice's. She steered them firmly back to the hedges, where they could not hear the two men talking.

"You two stay here," she said. "I know you would like to wander off and explore, but wait until we are finished." She smoothed her hair and went back to Father.

Almanzo crouched and scratched the dog's ears again. It rubbed its head against his knee and sat on his foot. They grinned at each other.

"That dog is rather smelly," Alice said, but she said it in a nice way. Eliza Jane would have scolded Almanzo for getting anywhere near it.

"He's still a good dog," Almanzo said. The

dog flopped onto its back and offered its belly for rubbing.

"What do you think?" Alice said, nodding at the land around them.

Almanzo ran his fingers through the dirt. "It looks pretty good. I'd plant wheat here, if it were my farm. Do you think Father will buy it? Do you think we're going to stay here?"

"Who knows?" Alice said. "Anything can happen, and most usually does."

"That sounds like something Royal would say," Almanzo said with a grin. "I bet he'd like this place. It's close enough to town for him to get a job there if he wanted." The dog butted his hand with its nose to make him keep scratching.

"Yes, and maybe Eliza Jane could teach at the school," Alice said. She made a face. "We'd better hurry up and graduate before she gets here!"

Almanzo laughed.

It seemed like they waited for a long time. Father stood with his arms crossed, listening to the farmer. He bent down and rubbed some of the dirt between his fingers. They walked along between the wheat. Finally they all came toward Almanzo and Alice. Almanzo stood up slowly. He didn't like the look of the strange farmer, or the way the farmer glared at the dog.

"We'll walk around and talk about it," Father was saying as they came up. He looked down at the dog, which was hiding behind Almanzo's legs. He glanced up at Almanzo. "Is this your dog?" he asked the farmer.

The man snorted. "It was here when I got here," he said. "And it won't go away. I've been thinking about drowning it."

Almanzo was horrified. Father tugged on his beard.

"Tell you what," the man said around the chunk of tobacco in his mouth, "you take the land, I'll throw in this good-for-nothing dog, too."

"Why don't we take him off your hands right now," Father said. It wasn't really a question.

The farmer shrugged.

"Suits me," he said.

Almanzo wanted to yell with excitement, but he knew he mustn't.

"What's his name?" he asked.

"Doesn't have one," said the farmer.

"You can call him anything you want, Almanzo," said Father. "He's yours now."

Almanzo looked down at the ground, hiding his smile. The dog looked up at him and wagged and wagged his back end like he knew what had happened.

Maybe he did, because when they left, the dog followed them. He didn't even look back at the farmer once. He stayed close to Almanzo's feet the whole way back to Uncle George's house.

"What are you going to call him, Manzo?" Alice asked.

"I don't know yet," Almanzo said.

"You'll have to keep him in the barn," Mother said. "I doubt Martha will want him in her house."

"Let's hope he can do something to earn his keep," Father said doubtfully.

"Like we have," Alice piped up. "Haven't we, Father? We help Uncle George and Aunt Martha all the time, don't we?" Almanzo thought she was right. Uncle George often had trouble lifting hay bales, and sometimes he had coughing fits that scared the cows. Almanzo and Father were able to finish all the farmwork much more quickly than he could by himself. And Mother was a much better cook than Aunt Martha. She and Alice kept the house as clean as their home in Malone, and Martha didn't look nearly as tired as she had when they'd arrived.

"I hope so," Father said, patting Alice's head. "But we are a lot of people in such a small space. If we buy this land, we can start building a new house for us to live in, so we can leave George and Martha in peace."

Almanzo held his breath. Did that mean they were moving here for certain? Could Starlight and Royal come join them soon?

"But already, James?" Mother said. "Shouldn't we think about it a bit longer?"

"This is a great opportunity, Angeline," Father said. "I believe Spring Valley could give us a farm even more prosperous than our home in Malone. The soil is richer, freshwater is everywhere, and the town is full of people like us, who want to build something new with their own hands."

Mother nodded thoughtfully. "I do like all the families we've met in town so far. It seems like a community we could be proud to be part of."

"I'm ready to decide," Father said. "I'd like to settle here. The sooner we have a new house built, the sooner Royal and Eliza Jane can join us. And if we buy this land, we'll be close enough to keep helping your brother as long as he is ill. If we don't take it now, we may have to live much farther away from them."

Almanzo felt guilty. He hadn't realized that Uncle George was really sick. He'd only been thinking about how strong and helpful he was, not about how weak and tired Uncle George was, or how much work it had been for Aunt Martha as well. What would George do without them if they went back to Malone? How would he run the farm?

"That is true," Mother said. "I just think, better be safe than sorry." Alice and Almanzo exchanged smiles. They had heard her say this many times before. And they knew what Father's response would be, too.

"Well, as I always say," Father said, "be sure you're right, then go ahead."

"Whatever you think best, James," Mother said. She squeezed his arm. "As long as we're all together, I know we can be happy anywhere."

Almanzo was sure now that Father would buy the land. This was it! They were really going to live in Spring Valley! Full of excitement, he ran through the trees and splashed into the stream. The dog ran along behind him, woofing a funny little woof that sounded like "Awwf! Awwf!"

Soon these fields would be theirs. Soon they

would have a new house of their own, and he would not have to sleep in the attic or be quiet all the time for Aunt Martha anymore.

Best of all, once their new farm was ready, it would be time for Royal and Starlight to come west as well.

LAST DAY OF SCHOOL

After Father bought the land, the rest of the summer flew by. Every day was filled with schoolbooks and ball games and chores for Uncle George, but whenever Almanzo had a moment, he ran with his dog down across the fields and over the stream to see the new house that was going up in the spot Father had chosen.

Wood shavings lay thick on the ground and sawdust drifted in the air. Father worked tirelessly from dawn to dusk. Mother often visited with Perley, and Father always listened to her ideas about how she wanted the kitchen to look and where they might put her loom.

Father wanted the house built so they could move in before winter. He had hired two men to work with him. They seemed friendly, but they made Almanzo feel shy. He had so many questions about what they were doing, but he was afraid to ask, so instead he watched and stayed out of the way.

Fat little Frank liked to sit on his foot, panting happily. Almanzo had decided to name the dog Frank after his cousin back home in Malone. He and Alice thought this was a fine joke. Cousin Frank loved to boast about what he could have and what he could do. He would be so puffed up and proud to hear that he had a namesake. It would be very funny to see his face if he ever met the odd-looking dog that was named after him.

Almanzo hoped that Cousin Frank and Uncle Wesley and Aunt Lindy would visit one day. He wanted to show off their beautiful land. Father kept saying he had never seen soil so rich, and there was so much of it! There were acres and acres to gallop across . . . once they had horses.

But before they could have horses, they needed a barn to keep them in. One day Father took Almanzo across to a plot he had cleared under the evergreens, not far from the house.

"This is where the barn will be," he said. He was building the house and barn close together so that he could build a covered walkway between them, like the one he had added to their New York home a few years earlier. If a mare gave birth in the middle of the night in the dead of frozen winter, it was much easier to go see to her without having to tramp through the piles of snow outside. There was also no danger of getting lost in a snowstorm on the way back. Father had heard many stories about the winter weather in Minnesota; it sounded as bad as the winters in upstate New York. He was determined to be prepared from the very beginning.

The hired men were starting to lay the foundation for the barn. It was going to be solid rock, strong and high, so that the animals would be safe from flooding and fierce blizzards. The tall roof would be supported by wide wooden beams. There would be stables for horses and pens for goats and chickens and cows—a place for all the farm animals they had at home.

"When are we going to bring everyone out from New York?" Almanzo asked. Father smiled at him, as if he knew that by "everyone" Almanzo really meant "Starlight."

"I want to get the house and barn built first," Father said, "so there's a place for all of us. Then selling the New York farm could take some time. And I don't want to leave your Uncle George alone until he is feeling better. So it may be a little while yet, Manzo."

Almanzo nodded. He understood all that. But he still hoped that it would happen soon. He hadn't seen Starlight in over half a year now. What if his horse forgot all about him?

Almanzo walked around the foundation, trying to imagine the rest of the barn going up. Which one would be Starlight's stall? Tall evergreens rose above him. One day he would be riding Starlight through these trees.

"Awwf!" Frank barked, as if he guessed what Almanzo was thinking.

"Sorry, Frank," he said, crouching to rub the dog's head. "I don't think you'll be able to keep up with us!"

With the fall came harvesttime and the end of the school term. Almanzo was glad he could put away his books for a few months, but he would miss Bert and playing ball with the boys in the schoolyard. He would also miss seeing Catherine in their music lessons. He had not found the courage to talk to her, but he hoped he would get the chance to one day.

On their last day of school, a missionary came to talk to the students about his work in India. The older classes crowded into the music room to hear him speak, because it was easier to fit them all in a space without desks. Miss

Lowe sat at her organ, listening quietly.

The missionary was tall and brown from the Indian sun. He joked about looking like the natives. Then he got very serious. He told them what important work the missionaries were doing. He told them about the long journey around the world. When he had first gone out to India, it had taken six months. His ship left from New York City, sailed south across the equator, around the bottom of South America, and then all the way across the Pacific to India. But his trip home only took two months, because of the new Suez Canal in Egypt. Now ships could go from India straight up to the Mediterranean Sea. From there the missionary had traveled over Europe to England and sailed home across the Atlantic Ocean from Liverpool.

Almanzo tried to picture the world map in his head. He could not believe people traveled so far. He had always learned about countries like India without thinking very much about them. They seemed far off, like history, or made up like the stories of Charles Dickens. It made him shiver to think there were boys just like him living halfway around the world in such a different kind of place. Boys who saw elephants and crocodiles and monkeys every day!

The missionary talked about how difficult it was to convince the heathens to become Christians. He said that if the students studied very hard and were very clever, they could join up and become missionaries, too. Missionaries had to be smart because not only did they write sermons and argue theology with the natives, they had to learn how to do it all in Hindustani, one of the main languages of India!

Almanzo had enough trouble writing compositions in English. He thought about asking if they had horses in India, but there was no time for questions. At the end the missionary passed around pamphlets and showed them a small stone statue he had brought back from India. He shook his head sadly as he said that it was one of the idols they worshipped.

After school was over, Alice stayed for a

few minutes to talk to her teacher about what she could read to study up for the next term. Almanzo went out to wait for her on the front steps. He saw that Catherine was out there as well, waiting for Bert. Her long hair swung in neat ringlets down her back to her slim waist. She was looking off at the edge of the sky.

It was already starting to get dark. Winter would be here before long, and the house was close to finished. Almanzo wondered if Catherine and her parents were going to live with Bert's family all winter.

This was his chance. He had to make himself speak to her.

"Hrm," he said, clearing his throat. "Um. Are you Bert's cousin?" The words came out in a rush. He had meant to say hello. He had meant to say, "You're Bert's cousin, aren't you?" He had not meant to stammer so much. Now he was sure he looked like a fool.

She turned her soft brown eyes to him. "Me? Yes, I am."

There was a pause that was even more

awkward than Almanzo had ever imagined such a moment could be. He scuffed his shoe along the step. Then Catherine smiled her dazzling sweet smile and he felt a little better.

"I'm Almanzo," he said. "Almanzo Wilder."

"What a funny name," she said. "Almanzo? Are you quite serious? I've heard Alice call you Mannie, but I thought it was short for something else, like Emanuel."

He had never really thought about his name very much. Although he had never met another Almanzo, he had also never met another Royal, or another Perley, or another Angeline like his mother. His name had never seemed any odder than anyone else's.

"Almanzo," Catherine said again. "Why, it's really outlandish."

"It's a family name," he said. "There is always an Almanzo in the Wilder family." He wanted to tell her the family legend about their ancestor who had gone to the Crusades. His life had been saved by an Arab named El Manzoor. Ever since then they had kept the name in the family—although changed a little bit—out of gratitude. Almanzo used to think it was a romantic story full of heroism and adventure, like *Ivanhoe*. Now it sounded plain peculiar. He couldn't bring himself to tell it.

"What about you?" he said, trying to change the subject.

"What about me?" she said with wide eyes.

"Do you, er, have any nicknames?" She stared at him blankly. "I mean—what do your friends call you?"

"They call me Catherine," she said as if it was obvious. "That's my name."

"Oh," Almanzo said, feeling small.

"India sounds horrible, doesn't it?" she offered with a shiver. "All those diseases and poor people."

"I guess," he said. "I'd like to see an elephant, though. I bet they're interesting."

"I bet they smell positively awful," Catherine said. "Even worse than cows and horses."

Almanzo was immensely relieved to see Alice coming out the front door. "All right, 'bye," he said in a rush.

"See you next term, Catherine!" Alice called as she took Almanzo's elbow. They went down the road, and Almanzo pulled out his handkerchief to mop his brow. He looked back and saw that Catherine was staring off at the sky again, winding a lock of hair around one finger.

"Oh no, you *don't*," Alice said, shaking his arm lightly. "Not you, too. All the boys are completely besotted with Catherine Baldwin."

"Bert isn't," Almanzo pointed out. Alice colored and tossed her curls.

"Well, perhaps he has some sense in that brain of his, then," she said. "That girl is a ninny."

"No, she's not," Almanzo said. "And I'm not besotted."

Alice rolled her eyes and patted his arm. "All right, dear."

Later, when Almanzo told his mother about the missionary's visit, she reminded him that he had an uncle who was also a missionary in India. Father's younger brother,

Royal, had gone out there with his wife in 1846. Royal and Eliza Jane were named after them. They had only been back once, when Almanzo was one year old. Other than that, they had been living in India for twenty-three years! Their children were cousins Almanzo had never met.

"We hope you will meet them one day," Mother said. "Your cousin Willy is one year younger than you. Sometimes missionaries send their children home to America to live with relatives and go to school here."

"Without their parents?" Almanzo asked, surprised. He could not imagine Father and Mother going away to India and leaving him behind for years and years. Their work was important to them, but family was most important of all.

"That's one of the sacrifices they must make to spread the good word," Mother said.

Almanzo thought that India sounded exciting to visit, but he was glad he lived in America. He would trade seeing an elephant any day for the chance to ride Starlight across the wide prairies he'd seen from the train. And now that the new house was almost built—perhaps he would get that chance soon!

CHRISTMAS IN THE
NEW HOUSE

It was a windy, crisp day in late autumn when
they were finally ready to move into their
new house. Almanzo could not believe that it
had been a whole year since they had gotten
the letter from Uncle George. One year ago,
he had been back in New York, dreading the
Academy. Now he was here in Spring Valley,
and perhaps in another year the whole family
would be here, too, including Starlight.

It did not take long to move their few things
out of Uncle George's house. Almanzo and his

father had spent several evenings and weekends building furniture for the new home, so there were beds and a table and chairs and dressers already waiting for them. Mother and Alice had sewn cheerful sky-blue curtains and new tablecloths and bedsheets. There was even a woven rag-carpet, like the ones they had at home, on the family room floor, where Perley sat and gurgled and tried to pull out all the colorful loops while the rest of the family unpacked.

Almanzo stood in his new room under the eaves and breathed in deeply. Frank sat at his feet, panting. His small tail thumped the smooth pine floorboards. The little dog wouldn't have to sleep in the barn anymore. He could come in the house and sleep next to Almanzo's bed now.

The smell of fresh-cut wood surrounded them, and Almanzo felt all the anxiety of living with Aunt Martha fade away. She had looked so relieved as they said good-bye that morning, but Almanzo thought he and Alice might be even happier than she was. They did not have to sleep in a hot stuffy attic anymore. They didn't even have to share a room. This new room would be his alone until Royal came out to join them. But that could be many months away still, as Father wanted to stay in Spring Valley for the fall wheat harvest and Mother did not like to travel in winter, and in any case Uncle George was still sick.

It was a strange Christmas that year, without Royal or Eliza Jane. At least their brother and sister did not have to have Christmas alone; they were going to Uncle Andrew's for Christmas dinner. But Almanzo still missed them, even Eliza Jane, and he knew that his mother was keenly sad that their whole family was not together for Christmas of all days.

Mother packed up a box of presents to send to New York. She worried that they might already have the things she bought for them. She was sure that the general store in Spring Valley must be years behind the stores in New York. What if Eliza Jane already had the collection of Charles Dickens stories *The Haunted House*? What if the hat Mother bought for Royal was already out of fashion?

She worried and fretted over the parcels until Father said gently that it was the sentiment of giving that counted, not the presents themselves. "That is what Christmas is all about," he said, and Mother couldn't disagree with that.

There was one present everyone was sure Royal and Eliza Jane would like, and that was a photograph of Perley. Mother wanted them to see how much bigger he'd grown, so she'd had it taken specially, although it was very hard to get the baby to sit still for it. In the photo Perley stared solemnly out with his big round eyes. It was a good photograph, but Almanzo wished there were a way to pack up and mail Perley's laugh for them, too. If you asked him, that was the best thing about his little brother.

Almanzo had carved a splendid whistle for Royal with his jackknife, but he could not think of a single thing to give Eliza Jane. He did not think she would want new ribbons, and Mother and Father had already bought her the nicest presents from the store. Anyway, he did not want to ask them for money. He wanted to think of something he could make himself.

Finally he had a brilliant idea. He could show Eliza Jane that he really was studying hard. He chose a composition he had written for Mr. Lloyd about the Shakespeare play *Richard III*. It was the best grade he had received all year. They had read the play aloud in class, which helped Almanzo to understand it. Some of the history was confusing to him, but he loved the line: "A horse! A horse! My kingdom for a horse!" He told Bert that he often felt that way, too—except that he had no kingdom to trade.

For three nights in a row Almanzo stayed up at his desk, working by the glow of the lamp. He wrote out the composition again in his neatest penmanship. He corrected all the mistakes that Mr. Lloyd had marked. He made it as perfect as he could. And then he dedicated it *To my sister Eliza Jane* and signed the bottom. Perhaps it was not a very exciting present, but he hoped it would show that he had thought about it and worked hard on it.

He read it over proudly, and then he started to worry. He had forgotten how much of the essay was about King Richard's horse. Maybe Eliza Jane would not like that. Maybe this would only prove to her that he thought about nothing but horses. Maybe she would tell him that he needed to get his head out of the stables and work harder. Or maybe she would just be disappointed that he had given her a school essay for Christmas.

But when he showed it to Alice the next morning, she said: "Oh, you beast! That's just perfect! I wish *I* had thought of it!"

"Really?" Almanzo said.

"Then I could have kept that lovely shawl for myself," Alice said wistfully. For the last month she had been knitting a soft shawl of a brown wool the color of Starlight's eyes. Now it was packed away with the other presents for New York.

"Eliza Jane will love the shawl," he reassured her.

"I *know* she will," Alice said. "*I* love it. But I made it for her, so I can't keep it. Anyway, I know she will love your present, too, Almanzo."

As they went to bed on Christmas Eve, Father joked, "Now, let's try to sleep a little later than half past three this year, all right?" He had said this every Christmas since Almanzo was nine. Almanzo could remember waking everyone up that year with his hooting and hollering. He had been so excited about Christmas, he hadn't even thought to check the time.

"I promise," Almanzo said with a yawn. He carried the candle up to his room and closed the door. It was so quiet without another person in there with him. He'd never gone to sleep alone on Christmas Eve before. He was glad that at least he had Frank, dozing on an old blanket on the floor beside him. Quickly he undressed, blew out the candle, and climbed into bed. Although he was nearly fifteen years old, he still felt as excited about Christmas as he had been when he was nine. He closed his eyes and tried hard to fall asleep.

To his surprise, the next thing he heard was a knock on his door and Frank barking. He sat up, feeling blurry-headed. He could smell pancakes. It was morning already!

"Almanzo, come on," Alice called through the door. "Merry Christmas!"

It was the first time Almanzo had not been the first person awake on Christmas morning. He hurried out of bed and splashed cold water on his face from the basin on his desk. Soon he and Frank were downstairs in the cozy warmth, and there was his sock, full and bulging like it was every Christmas morning.

"Look what I got!" Alice said, her eyes shining. She showed Almanzo a pair of kid gloves. They were milky white like cream and made from the softest leather. It felt like stroking a flower petal to touch them. Mother had given them to her in a box from the store so they would not be crumpled or ruined in her stocking.

"Merry Christmas, Almanzo," Mother said. "Open your presents and then run to do your chores. Breakfast is almost ready."

Almanzo dug into his sock happily. There was a packet of candy, as always, with warm yellow butterscotch circles and long red-and-white striped peppermint sticks. There was an orange, which must have cost extra to buy out here. And at the bottom of the sock there was a small lumpy cloth bag. Almanzo pulled it out and shook the contents into his hand.

"Marbles!" he said with delight. Many of the boys at school had marbles, but Almanzo had never been able to play because he had none of his own to bring to the game. Now he had ten! Some of them were a deep blue like the sky in the middle of summer. Two of them had a white stripe running through them. And one was dark midnight black with twinkling speckles all through it, as if someone had taken a night full of stars and rolled it into a little ball. They were all beautiful. Almanzo could have looked at them all day. But he had to hurry to the barn and do his chores.

"Thank you, Mother," he said, pouring the marbles back into the bag. "I can't wait to bring them to school."

"Almanzo's excited about school," Alice said. She had a streak of flour dust in her hair from helping with the pancakes. "Did you ever think you'd see the day, Mother?"

Almanzo's mother shook her head, smiling. "Well, I hoped for it!" she said. As Almanzo pulled on his boots, she added, "Now don't you linger in the barn. Come right back for breakfast."

Why would I linger in the barn? he wondered as he ran through the snow. Of course he wanted to hurry back for breakfast. Frank floundered along behind him. His legs were too short for the deep snowdrifts, but the little dog was determined to stay with Almanzo. He would appreciate the covered walkway once it was built!

Almanzo stopped in the doorway of the barn, stamping his feet. Suddenly his head jerked up. He heard a new sound—one he hadn't expected to hear in this barn for a few months yet. It sounded like a horse snorting.

He walked slowly down the row of unfin-ished stalls to the one at the end. Fresh hay covered the floor and fresh water rippled in the trough. A shape moved from the back of the stall to the front, and suddenly Almanzo was nose-to-nose with the most handsome horse he had seen since leaving Starlight.

Almanzo was speechless with delight. He stood still and let the horse sniff him. He could see that it was a young horse, maybe only a little older than a yearling. Finally the horse shook back its black mane and snorted in what Almanzo thought was an approving way.

"Well, I'll be," Almanzo said in amazement.

He heard laughing and clapping behind him. When he turned around, Mother and Father and Perley and Alice were all there between the barn doors, smiling broadly. Alice laughed again at the astonished expression on his face.

"Father!" Almanzo said. "There's a horse in here!"

Now Alice was laughing so hard she could barely stand.

"I know there is," Father said. "She's your Christmas present."

"She *is*?" Almanzo said wonderingly.

"I thought you might like something to keep you busy," Father said, his eyes twinkling. "And she was the finest horse at the market. Fine enough to breed with Starlight, perhaps, when we get him here."

Almanzo was too overwhelmed with joy to speak. But he knew that his father understood everything he was feeling inside.

"Horse!" Perley shouted, smacking his hands together. "Horse!" Perley did not know many words yet, but Almanzo thought it was a very good sign that one of them was "horse."

"All right, now breakfast," Mother said.

"Can't I stay with her? Just for a minute?" Almanzo asked.

"No," Mother said firmly. "I know you will spend the rest of the day in here, so we'll start with a proper family breakfast, and then you may be excused."

Almanzo wolfed down his mountain of pancakes drizzled with golden maple syrup. He ate his bacon faster than he had ever eaten, and he didn't even taste his milk as he drank it. Finally Mother let him go back to his new horse.

He stayed in the barn almost the entire day, letting the filly get used to him. She seemed gentle and good-natured. Her name was Queen, and she had been raised by a man that Father trusted to be good with horses. Almanzo couldn't wait to tell Royal. At last he had something to write in his letters! He would have to tell his brother to tell Starlight all about Queen.

"Maybe one day you'll have a son with Starlight, and I can name him Prince," Almanzo said to her. She whinnied as if that idea sounded fine to her.

Uncle George and Aunt Martha came over for supper, so Almanzo had to go back into the house, but first Uncle George came out to see the new horse. He coughed a lot and he hunched forward when he walked, like something in his chest hurt. The doctor in town did not know what was wrong with him. None of the medicine he'd given Uncle George seemed to help.

But his eyes shone as he looked at Queen, and Almanzo could see something in Uncle George that was just like Almanzo and Father—someone who loved to farm. It was sad that he was so sick that he could not give all his energy to his farm, as he wanted to.

Almanzo hoped that Uncle George would get well soon for two reasons. Of course he wanted his uncle to feel better and stronger and happier. He also knew they could not go home to get the others until George was well. He didn't mind working on both farms at once; he liked to be helpful and busy. But it was hard waiting and not knowing when things would change.

Alice and Almanzo were both nervous about how Aunt Martha would be at supper, but she seemed like a whole new person now that they were not living in her house anymore. She even laughed a few times. She complimented Mother's pumpkin pie, and she had brought baked sweet potatoes with brown sugar to add to the meal as well. They were warm and delicious and almost melted away in Almanzo's mouth.

Most surprising of all, when Perley came over to show her his new toy, she picked him up and sat him in her lap.

"How very clever," Aunt Martha said, studying the toy horse. "You carved this for him, Almanzo?"

Almanzo nodded, pleased.

Perley reached up and patted Aunt Martha's sandy brown hair. She smiled and gave him a little squeeze. "I can't believe how big he's getting," she said to Mother.

"Eating a lot and growing fast, just like Almanzo at that age," Mother said proudly.

Aunt Martha let Perley take her hand and play with it, turning it over between his chubby fingers. Her smile seemed a little sad to Almanzo. "I hope someday—" she said, and then stopped. "Well, it would make life bright to have children like yours."

Mother's eyes shone as she looked around at her family. "It does," she said. "Don't worry, Martha. Once George is well again, you will have plenty of time to start a family of your own."

Martha moved her shoulders a little, as if she wasn't so sure. Then she set Perley back down on the floor to play with his toy, and she turned the conversation back to Mother's pumpkin pie.

After everyone had gone and the supper dishes were done, Father settled Perley on his lap to read him a storybook. Almanzo and Alice and Mother sat quietly by the fire, making popcorn and playing the new card game Alice had got in her stocking. It was called "Authors." The front of the little box said AUTHORS in bright red letters. There was a drawing of a marble bust of a bearded man on a table with a pile of books. Behind it you could see a group of young people laughing and playing with the cards.

Each card had a drawing of an author on it and the name of three books he had written. Every author had four cards in the stack, and the idea was to get all four cards to make a set. The person with the most matching sets would win the game.

Alice dealt out all the cards between the three of them. Almanzo had three of the Shakespeare cards right from the start: Shakespeare, *Merchant of Venice*, and *King Lear*. He was glad to see an author he recognized. Some of the others did not seem familiar at all. He began by asking Mother if she had the fourth Shakespeare card, *Hamlet*. She did, so she had to give it to him, and then he had one matching set already. He laid it down on the table proudly.

Then he could go again, because he had won a card. He asked Alice if she had *Waverley* by Sir Walter Scott. He had *Ivanhoe* and he could see from the list on the card that the third book was *Marmion*, but he wasn't sure he could pronounce that one right. Alice didn't have "Waverley," so then it was Mother's turn.

Mother quickly got a set of an author called Robert Burns. The books were *Tam O'Shanter*, *Bannockburn*, and *Auld Lang Syne*. Almanzo had never read or even heard of any of those books.

"What does 'auld lang syne' mean?" he asked his mother. "Is it someone's name?"

"It means long ago, in the old days," Mother said. "It's a song that people sometimes sing to celebrate the new year. I didn't know that Robert Burns wrote it."

"He wrote the poem," Alice said. "Someone else put it to music. We learned that at the Academy." She took *Waverley* from Mother and *Ivanhoe* from Almanzo to make the Sir Walter Scott set.

The fire flickered and crackled behind them, casting a warm orange glow over the cards in their hands. Outside snow was falling again, carpeting the world in a thick white blanket like the one Mother had woven Father for Christmas. The buttery, salty smell of the crisp popcorn filled the cozy room, mingling with the familiar smell of Father's pipe. Father rocked in his chair with Perley on his knee, watching them play. The firelight seemed to hold them all together in a bright circle, chasing the shadows into the corners.

Almanzo thought of the glossy brown horse with the shining eyes that was waiting for him in the stable. He reached down to rub Frank's ears and looked around at his family, warm and safe in their own home. Even without Royal and Eliza Jane, it was still a grand Christmas.

A DEATH IN THE FAMILY

It was a cold, wet day in early March. A rainstorm had blown through in the morning, soaking the ground and leaving the bare trees dripping big, fat, cold droplets or little showers of freezing spray. Tiny raindrops clung to the branches, spaced out and glittering like diamonds in a jeweler's window. A fine mist hung in the air, blurring the edges of things. It was more than cold, because the dampness took the cold all the way into your bones and made you feel you might never be dry again.

Almanzo rode slowly through the stand of trees, hearing the mud squish under Queen's hooves. Rain dripped off the brim of his hat, and the tip of his nose was bright red from the cold. Queen's sleek black mane hung limply, and she would sometimes swing her head around to look at him, as if she blamed herself for making him come out in such weather.

"It's all right, Queenie," Almanzo said, patting her neck. "We'll head back to the warm stable soon." Father had asked him to ride over to Uncle George's and make sure that they had enough firewood up at the house.

Almanzo had heard his parents talking about Uncle George's illness in low voices. They were still waiting for him to get better so they could go home to Malone and sell the farm there. Mother was worried about leaving her brother on his own. He was already working too hard for someone so weak, even with Almanzo and Father doing all they could to help.

But they had been in Spring Valley for a

year now. In his letters, Royal sounded restless and discontented. He did not want to be running a farm; he wanted to be learning how to be a storekeeper. Father needed to go back and prepare everything for the move, which would also take a long time. He was starting to think he shouldn't wait until Uncle George was well again, since no one knew how long that might take.

Almanzo sometimes felt as if they had been in Spring Valley forever. Father had bought a new pair of horses to pull their buggy, and the barn was full of chickens clucking and flapping and the soothing murmur of cows breathing and chewing. There was always more work to do, especially with Uncle George's farmwork added on.

The town of Spring Valley was getting bigger all the time, too. New stores kept appearing all along Broadway, and Mother already had an account to sell her butter and eggs at J. C. Halbkat's grocery. The large building that was just a foundation when they'd arrived was now finished and called Parson's Stone Block. New settlers arrived in town every day. Perhaps Spring Valley was more like Malone than the remote pioneer town Almanzo had expected, but it was full of the excitement of new growth and ambitious enterprise, which Almanzo and Father both loved.

Mother and Father had even found friends who were interested in sponsoring the building of a new Methodist church together. For the time being, the congregation met in the upstairs hall at Parson's Stone Block, but one day they hoped to build a tall, beautiful Gothic church with stained-glass windows.

Sometimes Almanzo worried that he'd forgotten what Starlight looked like. Other times he worried that Starlight would like Royal more than him by the time he got back. He was very glad to have Queen to take his mind off all his worrying.

He was not far from the stream when he saw a figure moving through the trees. It moved in a strange, lurching way, like it was pushing itself from one tree to the next. He squinted and rubbed the water out of his eyes, but the fog made it hard to see. He wondered if he should go back and get Father, but the thought made him feel cowardly. He was full fifteen years old now, big and strong for his age from all the work he did. Even if the stranger was a vagabond, there was only one of him.

He nudged Queen forward until he could see the person clearly.

Her hair was loose and clung wetly to her face. She was not wearing a hat, or gloves, or a coat, or even a wrap. She was shaking and staring with a lost look on her face. She did not seem to notice Almanzo as he rode closer. With a start, he finally recognized her.

"Aunt Martha!" he called, bringing Queen to a halt. He swung down and walked closer, leading the horse behind him. His aunt's green eyes were as empty and far away as the moon. He took one of her hands in his.

"Aunt Martha, are you all right? What's wrong?"

She didn't answer, so he pulled off his coat and put it around her. The cold air hit his arms and back as if he weren't wearing a shirt at all. He wound his long muffler around her face and tugged his hat down on her head. All of his things seemed so big on her. Had he grown taller, or had she shrunk?

"I'll take you home," he said, gently turning her back to the stream. "Uncle George will take care of you."

This revived her for a moment. "What nonsense," she snapped. "He's dead. What can he do?"

Almanzo didn't know what to say. How could Uncle George be dead? Almanzo had seen him only yesterday. He had seemed no different than usual.

"I didn't think he would ever *die*," Aunt Martha said in a quieter voice. She leaned against Almanzo's shoulder and he guided her over to Queen. He braced his hands on her waist and lifted her onto the horse. She huddled into his coat without speaking. He wrapped the reins around his hand and led Queen back through the bare, wet trees and across the muddy fields to his house, where a lamp was burning brightly in the window.

By the time they reached the barn Almanzo was shivering badly, but he kept going, one foot in front of the other. Mother must have seen him through the kitchen window, because the door flew open as he got closer. Mother and Alice came running onto the front porch.

"Mercy on us, Almanzo!" Mother gasped. "What happened to your coat?" She hurried up to him, wrapping her shawl around his shoulders. Then she saw the woman on the horse behind him. "Martha?"

"Uncle George is dead," Almanzo said through chattering teeth.

Mother's face seemed to fold in on itself like paper getting wet. Alice's hands flew to her mouth. Almanzo wondered if he looked that pale, too.

Mother and Almanzo helped Martha down from the horse and led her up to the house. In the doorway, Alice knelt to take off Martha's shoes for her and then hurried upstairs to find a pair of dry wool socks. Mother took Martha into the sitting room while Almanzo went back out to unsaddle and stable Queen. He was old enough to know that horses had to be taken care of, no matter what.

When he came back inside, little puddles of muddy water from Martha's dress had dripped a trail through Mother's clean kitchen and into the sitting room. Martha was sitting in one of the rocking chairs by the fire. She held a steaming cup of coffee between her shaking hands. Alice's thick blue shawl and Mother's good red one were wrapped around her shoulders, and her feet were resting on a warm flatiron. Father and Mother were standing beside her, looking very solemn. Even Perley, sitting on the rug with his blocks, was quiet and serious, although he was too young to understand what was happening.

"He was sick for so long," Martha said, gazing into the cup. "When nothing changed, I thought he was going to stay sick forever. I thought it was just his constitution. I didn't— I didn't think he would go ahead and die like that."

"You've had quite a shock, Martha," Father said kindly.

"But we're here to look after you," Mother said. "That's what family is for. We will make sure that you're all right." There was a wobble in her strong, gentle voice.

"And of course you must stay here tonight," Father said. "I can go into town and make arrangements for the funeral."

Almanzo realized that Aunt Martha was crying. He'd thought at first that her face was just wet from the rain, but now he could see tears spilling down her cheeks. In her own way she must have cared about Uncle George. He felt guilty for all the unkind thoughts he had ever had about her.

"Almanzo," Father said seriously, "I want you to go over and take care of George's livestock. Do all his chores as usual. Do not go into the house. I'll meet you at his barn."

Almanzo nodded, feeling chilled. He didn't want to go into their house and see Uncle George's body. He had never seen a dead body. His grandparents on his father's side had died before he was born. He was too young to remember his other grandfather, who died when he was four. And he only had vague memories of his grandmother's funeral when he was eleven. He remembered wearing his good dark suit and sitting still on the hard benches of the church for a long time while the preacher spoke. It had been a lot like a Sunday.

But now he was fifteen, nearly old enough to have his own farm. He squared his shoulders. He would not be afraid. If Royal were here, he'd be the one to help Father with everything. But now it was up to Almanzo.

Uncle George's farm was quiet and deserted. Even the chickens were inside their coop with their heads tucked under their wings. The light misty rain was still drifting down in soft gusts and flurries.

Almanzo did the chores carefully and thoroughly. He made sure that all the hay on the floor of the barn was new and sweet-smelling. He brushed down Uncle George's horses until they glowed in the lamplight. He pumped new water for the cows' drinking trough. While he worked, he thought about how they would have to write to Eliza Jane and Royal to tell them what had happened. His brother and sister hadn't really known Uncle George, but he was sure they would feel sad anyway.

He was nearly finished when he heard the sound of wheels outside. Father pulled up to the barn with a load of lumber in the wagon behind him and two strange men on the seat next to him. Both men wore dark suits and had long, sallow faces. They looked like father and son. The older man was carrying a large black case on his lap. Almanzo guessed that he must be the undertaker.

As they climbed down, he realized that the younger one was probably his own age, if not younger. He thought how lucky he was that his father was a farmer, and that he did not have to be apprenticed in a trade like undertaking.

Almanzo went to unload the lumber while Father took the undertakers inside the house. He could guess what the wood was for without being told. They were going to build Uncle George's coffin.

He laid out the long, flat boards on the clean, dry floor of the barn. The smell of fresh sawdust tickled his nose. The smoky gray barn cat came and sat beside him. She meowed loudly, and Almanzo imagined that she was asking, "What will become of me?" He did not know. He didn't know what would happen to Uncle George's farm without him there to run it. Would Aunt Martha live on it alone?

He set out a hammer and nails. He measured the boards and cut them to be the same length, six feet long. He sanded down the splinters and rough edges and bumps in the wood. He kept his mind fixed on the feel of the grain under his fingers. If he concentrated on building, he would not have to think about Uncle George being dead.

In all the time they had been there, Almanzo had always expected his uncle to get better. He'd been waiting for it anxiously. He'd never imagined this might happen instead.

Father did not say anything when he came out of the house, but he nodded approvingly at what Almanzo had done. He took a small brown paper bag out of his pocket. Inside were three hinges that he had bought at the general store. Almanzo helped attach them to form a lid for the coffin.

It was dark when they finished. Almanzo realized that he had not eaten since breakfast. He felt too tired and sad to be hungry.

The undertakers came out of the house. "We're ready to move the body into the coffin," said the older one.

"Wait," said a new voice. They turned to see a lantern coming up the path from the fields. It was a moment before they saw the person holding it, and another moment before they realized that it was Almanzo's mother. She was carrying a bundle of fabric under her arm.

"Angeline," Father said, "you don't have to—"

"It's for the coffin," she said, holding out the fabric. "He shouldn't have to lie in a plain box like that. It isn't right. I just want to line it so he'll be more comfortable."

Father opened his mouth to speak, and then he closed it again. He nodded and took her into the barn. Almanzo followed and watched as she shook out the fabric. He recognized the wine-colored wool from one of Mother's good dresses, and he saw that she had cut it up to make the lining with. It was her gift to her brother. She tucked the fabric into the box until it covered the bottom.

"All right," she said, picking up the lantern. "Now it's ready."

"Almanzo, please escort your mother home," Father said. "I'll drive the coffin to the mortuary, where they'll hold it until the funeral service. The minister said he would arrange it."

"We should put a notice in the paper," Mother said. She smoothed down her skirts and blinked as if she was trying not to cry.

"I'll see to it," Father said. "Go on home and

rest." He put one hand on Almanzo's shoulder. "Take care of everything at home until I get there."

"Yes, Father," Almanzo said. He took his mother's elbow and they went out of the barn together. He looked back once at the pine box sitting empty on the floor, open and waiting. A shiver ran through him that was not from the cold weather.

Outside, he held the lantern high so they could see the dips and turns of the dirt path ahead of them. Thick clouds covered the sky, hiding the moon and the stars.

It had been a long, sad day, and there were still the chores on their own farm to be done before he could go in for supper. Almanzo felt older than he had that morning. He felt as if he had stepped over a line he hadn't known was there, from being a boy into being a man.

Good-bye, Uncle George, he thought. *We will all miss you.*

THE BASKET SOCIAL

After the sorrow of Uncle George's death, it was a relief when school started again, and all of a sudden there seemed to be a sociable or a dance or a church meeting every other week. Almanzo did not go to all of them—he had too much work to do on both farms—but Alice went as often as she could and always came home glowing and full of stories.

Father had not said anything about going home to Malone yet. Almanzo knew they couldn't leave Aunt Martha to handle the farm on her own. They had promised to stay and help her as long as she needed them. So he wasn't sure what would happen next.

It was especially strange because after all the time they had spent living at Aunt Martha's, now she seemed to be always at their home. Almanzo was not surprised that his mother was far more welcoming than Aunt Martha had been. Mother loved to be helpful, and she especially loved having other people around.

Aunt Martha worked hard to keep her farm going, but she ate most meals with the Wilders, helped with the cooking and cleaning, and played in the sitting room with Perley while Mother did her weaving. She even slept on a pallet in the sitting room sometimes when it was too cold or rainy to walk home. She seemed lost and a little sad in her black mourning dress, but each day she smiled more, and after a while she began going to the sociables and church meetings with Alice. There was a man with a pair of white horses who sometimes drove her home, and then Martha would be happy the rest of the evening.

At school Almanzo struggled to keep up with his lessons, played ball and marbles with the other boys, and stole secret glances at Catherine every chance he got. She had gotten even prettier since that day he had first seen her on the train platform. Although many of the boys were sweet on her, Almanzo could not tell whether she liked any of them. She behaved exactly the same with everybody.

One Monday Mr. Lloyd came into the organ room shortly before the end of the music lesson. Miss Lowe gave a little jump when she saw him, and then signaled for everyone to stop singing.

"My apologies, Miss Lowe," Mr. Lloyd said politely. "I have an announcement to make, and I thought it would be best to share it with all the classes at once."

Miss Lowe nodded and went to sit down at her organ again. She was always very quiet. Almanzo had only ever heard her talk about music. In the mornings he saw her hurry into the schoolhouse and go straight to the organ. In the afternoons she left right after their lesson. He often saw her leaving from the windows upstairs, as he stared out into the golden daylight, wishing he were outdoors. He had never even seen her speak to another teacher.

"As many of you know," Mr. Lloyd said, "some of the teachers have been working for a while on getting this school a proper library. We've decided to hold a fund-raising event that we think you'll enjoy." He paused, smiling at their curious faces. "On Saturday, we will have a basket social here in the schoolhouse. I hope you'll all attend, and ladies, of course, please bring well-filled baskets to auction off." He wagged one finger at them. "Remember not to reveal which basket is yours!"

That day after school, Almanzo asked Bert, "What is a basket social?"

"Miss Wilder," Bert said to Alice, "I am astonished and perplexed at the ignorant state of your brother. Have you no sense of responsibility for his edification?" Bert loved using big words around Alice, since she always knew what they meant.

"It's not *my* fault!" she protested. "All he ever thinks about is horses." They were standing by the hitching post as Bert untied Velvet. Almanzo dug into his pocket, pulled out a bit of carrot, and slipped it to Velvet while his companions argued.

"A basket social, my good man," Bert said, "is a time-honored event full of mischief and deception and victuals and inevitable misunderstandings and recriminations. It's great fun, you'll see."

"Well, I'm sure that helps him," Alice said, putting her hands on her hips. "Manzo, the idea of a basket social is that each girl packs a picnic basket with enough food inside for two people. At the social, the baskets are auctioned off, and the highest bidder on each one gets the basket."

"*And*," Bert said, "the important part is that he gets to eat the food inside the basket with the girl who made it."

Almanzo's heart thumped in his chest. What if he bought Catherine's basket? Did he dare to go on a picnic with her? But surely every boy in school would be vying for her basket. He could not possibly have enough money to beat them all.

"No, Bert, the *important* part is that nobody knows which basket is whose," Alice said. "There are no names on them. A boy could easily bid on the wrong basket and end up escorting the wrong girl to a picnic, which anyone can see would be a disaster."

"His sweetheart would never forgive him," Bert said. "That is where the recriminations come in. It would be so much easier if she would just tell him ahead of time which basket to choose."

"Of course, a *smart* boy would be able to figure out the right basket without being told," Alice said. "If he *pays attention*."

Almanzo often got the feeling that Bert and Alice were having another conversation underneath the one he was hearing. But it was not his business to figure it out.

Besides, perhaps Alice was right. Perhaps he could guess Catherine's basket. If he was the only one who guessed it, perhaps he wouldn't have to compete with the other boys for it. And then he'd have a whole Saturday afternoon to spend with her, just the two of them.

All that week Mother and Alice talked about the basket social. Mother had never been to one, and she wasn't sure that it sounded entirely proper, but since it was for the library, she finally agreed that Alice could bring a basket to auction. Then they talked for ages about what to pack in it, until Almanzo's dreams were full of food and he woke up starving every morning.

On Saturday morning, Almanzo took his wallet from the drawer in his desk and counted out the money he had saved. He went into the kitchen and saw Alice's basket sitting on the table. Alice whirled around from the oven.

"Almanzo!" she protested. "You're not supposed to know which one is mine!"

"Wouldn't you rather I knew?" he pointed out. "So I won't accidentally bid on it? What would the other girls say if you had to have a picnic with your own brother?"

Alice tossed her head, thinking. "Well," she said. "I wouldn't mind picnicking with you. But I suppose you're right." She bent down to the oven and took out the pound cake she had made. It was dense and golden and perfect-looking. She wrapped it in a clean red-and-white checkered cloth and put it gently in the basket.

Almanzo peeked inside. The basket was lined with a pretty white silk square embroidered around the edges with cheerful buttercups. Besides the pound cake, there were two thick and juicy pork loin sandwiches with homemade crab-apple jelly, a small bag of chewy chocolate cookies, a jar of dried fruit, two apples, and two bottles of sweet, tangy lemonade that Alice had made herself.

"Wow," he said. "Maybe I do want to win your basket."

Alice beamed. "Do you think he'll like it?"

"Who?" Almanzo asked.

"Um—whoever wins my basket, of course," Alice said quickly.

"Absolutely," he said. "He'll be a very lucky guy."

Alice shook out another red-and-white cloth to cover the food with. Then she untied the ribbon from her hair. She had worn the same ribbon all week. It was a deep, rich gold color that brought out the gold highlights in her brown hair. It was bordered with a shimmery copper-colored thread. Alice tied the ribbon around the handle of the basket and arranged it into a pretty bow.

Suddenly Almanzo realized something.

"You did that on purpose!" he cried. "You wore that ribbon all week and now you're putting it on the basket so that someone will know it's yours!"

Alice turned very, very pink. "No, I'm not!" she said. "I mean, there's no someone!" She stamped her foot. "I mean—all the girls do this, Mannie! It's our little trick. That's how we know if the boys are paying attention. For instance, Peter Merritt has been walking Sally Lobdill home from school every day, but Sally says that if he can't find her basket by the blue ribbon she's been wearing, then she'll know that he doesn't really care for her."

"What?" Almanzo said. "That's crazy."

"It's not crazy, it's perfectly sensible. That's how girls think," Alice said. She went over to the looking glass in the hall and began unbraiding her hair.

"Then girls are crazy," Almanzo said. "Boys never notice ribbons. It doesn't mean he doesn't like her." After all, he liked Catherine very much, but he had no idea what color her ribbons were.

"Sally thinks it does," Alice said, combing her hair and pinning it up. "So do lots of girls." Her deft fingers quickly fixed her hair into what Almanzo guessed was the latest fashionable style. He was glad he didn't have to worry about such things. He only had to slick back his hair and comb it down, and he was finished. He did not have to think about ribbons and matching colors and how wide a skirt should be. And he did not have crazy notions about how to tell if someone liked you.

He was lucky to be a boy.

The schoolhouse was packed with students when they got there. Alice had thrown her shawl over her basket to keep it hidden. As they walked up the front steps, three other girls from her class swept up to her, giggling, and they all vanished into the classroom where the baskets were to be set out.

Almanzo stood awkwardly near the entrance, feeling again like it was the first day of school. The building seemed different. Everyone was dressed in their nicest clothes and seemed more grown up than usual. Long tables were set up in the hall with pitchers of lemonade and plates of cookies sprinkled with pink sugar. He took a cookie and stood against the wall, trying to look like he wasn't so out of place.

The hall seemed to be full of girls chattering and townsfolk that he did not know. But finally Joshua and Victor found him, and they joked about whether they could get a whole picnic for a nickel. Then Mr. Lloyd announced that they could go in to see the baskets on display.

There were two baskets on each desk. Almanzo was astonished at how different they all looked. Some of them had lots of ribbons tied on the handle. Some of them were draped in colorful cloth. Some were big and some were small. One even had a little rag doll tucked into the corner, grinning a stitched-on smile.

They were allowed to peek in the baskets as long as they did not take anything or disturb the decorations. Almanzo looked around the room, wondering. Which one was Catherine's?

He tried desperately to remember what kind of ribbons she had worn that week. Were they pink? She often wore pink. Several of the baskets had pink ribbons, but one basket was nearly covered in them, all around the handle and woven into the wicker of the frame. The ribbons were wide and made of a pale pink lace. They matched the roses embroidered on the tablecloth and napkins that were neatly folded into the basket. A lot of boys kept walking by and looking at it. Were they thinking the same thing as Almanzo?

Almanzo went over and peeked inside the pink basket. There was a white paper bag of store-bought candy. There was a tin of store-bought sardines and a loaf of plain whole wheat bread to put them on. There were two bottles of ginger ale, the new drink Almanzo had seen at the general store. He wondered if it tasted like the ginger water his mother made.

It didn't look anywhere near as appealing as Alice's basket. The outside was very pretty, but inside it seemed as if the basket maker had spent very little time preparing a delicious meal. Although the ribbons looked right, he found it hard to believe that Catherine would have put together such a dull lunch.

He looked around and spotted a basket sitting by itself on a desk at the back. It looked very forlorn. A thin, black braided ribbon hung from the handle. It wasn't even tied in a bow. The basket was small and ragged with a few tiny holes in it. The white napkin lining the inside was plain cotton with an uneven edge. But when he looked inside, the food looked very good—fried chicken and doughnuts and sweet plums and a whole miniature chocolate layer cake. Almanzo's stomach growled at the sight of it, even though he had eaten a good breakfast.

He wondered who had made it. He did not know most of the girls in school very well. They always stayed inside talking while the boys played outside. It could also be from one of the young ladies from town. He had seen several people in the hall who were a little too old for school anymore. Could it belong to one of them?

He looked around, but there were no girls in the room. Some of them were clustered in the doorway, watching and whispering and laughing behind their hands. But they whisked out of sight when any of the boys looked at them.

Perhaps this was a riddle. Maybe Catherine had made a basket that looked nothing like her, because she wanted the boy who won her basket to see her the way she really was. Maybe she knew that all the foolish boys would bid on a frilly, pretty basket. Maybe she would be impressed if he was the only one to figure out which one was really hers.

A hand grabbed his sleeve and yanked him into the corner of the room.

"All right," Bert said in his ear. "I confess. I'm beat. I surrender."

"Surrender?" Almanzo echoed.

"I can't figure it out!" Bert cried. He clutched his hair. "I've looked into every basket in here, and I don't see a single clue! I have no idea! What kind of girl makes apple turnovers? Who likes cold boiled potatoes? Should I see her name spelled out in blueberries at the bottom of the basket? I don't know how we're supposed to know!" He threw up his hands. "I'm a smart guy, aren't I, Almanzo?"

"You are," Almanzo consoled him. "But we don't think like girls do. Whose basket are you looking for?" He was pretty sure he could guess.

"Well—anyone's," Bert said, blushing. "I mean, if there's any way to figure it out, I'd like to know, wouldn't you?"

Almanzo looked between the pink beribboned basket and the lonely one in the back. He *would* like to know.

"I just need a hint," Bert said. "Something to start me off. For instance, say . . . do you know which one is your sister's?"

Almanzo nearly laughed. For a smart guy, Bert was not very good at hiding his feelings. "I'm not sure it would be fair to tell you," he said. Did Alice want Bert to bid on her basket? Sometimes it seemed as if she didn't like him at all. But she was a girl, and girls could be confusing. Maybe that was exactly what she wanted.

"Please, my friend." Bert abandoned any attempt to seem casual and clasped his hands together pleadingly. "I'm a stand-up fellow, honest. I'll have her home before supper. And what'll happen to me if I get it wrong? Can you imagine the trouble I'd be in?"

Almanzo remembered what Alice had said about Sally and Pete. He wished he was brave enough to ask Bert if he knew which basket was Catherine's. "All right," he said. "I'll show you." He led the way over to Alice's pretty, fall-colored, friendly-looking basket.

"Pound cake!" Bert said rapturously. "I *love* pound cake!"

"You still have to win the auction," Almanzo reminded him. And so did he, if he wanted to win the picnic with Catherine. Was he really brave enough to bid on either of the two baskets?

"Oh, I will win it," Bert said. "You bet your boots!"

THE AUCTION

Mr. Lloyd rang a small bell and announced that anyone who wished to bid on a basket should go into the music room. Bert grabbed Almanzo's arm and dragged him along. They squeezed into a space by the wall where they had a good view of the front of the room. It seemed like every young man in Spring Valley was crammed into that room. Almanzo knew there were not enough baskets for all of them.

He began to feel queasy. He had five dollars in his wallet. But surely he could not spend all five dollars on a basket—especially when he was not sure which girl it belonged to!

"Miss Thayer has graciously agreed to be our auctioneer," Mr. Lloyd said. Alice's teacher stepped behind the lectern that had been set up at the front of the room. She arranged a small gavel and a glass of water in front of her as Mr. Lloyd withdrew.

"All right, ladies and gentlemen," Miss Thayer said. "Let's all have a lovely time. The first basket, please!"

Two of the girls carried in a sweet little basket with a posy of wildflowers wound into the handle. Almanzo was sure it was not Catherine's, but he liked the look of it. He was pleased when his friend Joshua won the basket. Miss Thayer wrote down Joshua's name as the girls carried the basket out.

But Almanzo was dismayed to see how the auction worked. Miss Thayer would say, "Do I hear ten cents for this charming basket?" Then a boy would yell, *"Ten cents!"* and then another boy would yell *"Fifteen cents!"* and then all the boys seemed to start shouting at once. It was hard to see how Miss Thayer could keep track of all the bids flying through the air. But somehow she seemed sure that Joshua had bid the most, at a dollar and a quarter.

More baskets came out. Most of them sold for around a dollar. That seemed like a lot to Almanzo, but it was much less than five dollars. Perhaps he could afford Catherine's basket after all.

Alice's basket came in.

"What a lovely treat this basket is," said Miss Thayer. "Pound cake and lemonade and all kinds of nice things. Who would like to bid ten cents?"

Bert raised his hand. "Ten cents!" he called out. Almanzo glanced around and saw Alice peeking in at the door. He couldn't tell if she looked pleased.

"Fifteen cents!" said a boy near the back of the room.

Before Bert could speak, another boy said, "Twenty cents!"

And then a third boy called out, "Thirty cents!"

"Thirty-five!" said the one at the back of the room.

"Forty cents!"

"Fifty cents!"

"Fifty-five!"

"Three dollars!" Bert bellowed frantically. A hush fell over the room. Everyone turned to stare at him. Bert was beet red. Almanzo thought that if that was him, he'd want to sink right into the floor and disappear.

"Three dollars!" Miss Thayer said in delight. "How wonderful! Are you sure?" A few of the girls at the door nudged Alice, who had hidden her face in her hands. Almanzo didn't know if that was a good sign or a bad sign.

Bert lifted his chin. "Yes, ma'am," he said.

"Very well!" Miss Thayer said, banging her gavel. "Sold, for three dollars, to the *exceptionally* charming young Mr. Baldwin."

"Whew," Bert whispered, sagging against the wall as the next basket was brought in. "I hope you weren't lying to me, Manzo. That would be a very cruel joke."

"There is no need to play jokes on you," Almanzo said, "when you are quite amusing enough on your own."

"Oh, ha ha," Bert said, but he was grinning from ear to ear.

A few baskets later, in came the one festooned with pink lacy ribbons. It seemed like every young man in the room sat forward when they saw it. Almanzo's face was prickling with heat.

He was right to worry. Almost as soon as Miss Thayer began to speak, someone called out "Twenty cents!" And then the bids began to fly, fast and furious. Almanzo could not keep up with them. He couldn't even open his mouth before a new number was shouted out.

The amount climbed higher and higher. Even the girls at the door looked horrified when it passed six dollars. Almanzo shook his head. He couldn't buy it now, even if he wanted to. He had to hope that it was not

Catherine's basket after all, and that all the other boys were wrong.

He hoped so even more when he saw who won the basket—swaggering, mean-eyed, redheaded Eddie. He beat all the other boys with an eight-dollar bid. Almanzo could hardly believe it. He wondered if Eddie had even looked in the basket. You could buy all the things that were in there for much less than eight dollars. You could not buy Catherine's company, that was true. But it would serve Eddie right if the basket turned out to belong to a dull girl instead.

The last basket to come out was the sad little one with the black ribbon. The girl who brought it in kept frowning as if she was very disappointed in it. It looked even more sad after the parade of cheery, colorful ones that came before it.

"Oh," Miss Thayer said. She peeked at the food inside. "Well, this one does look delicious, gentlemen. It's not often you see a chocolate layer cake in one of these!" She smiled a little too brightly. "Do I hear ten cents for this—for this basket?"

An awful silence settled over the classroom. Nobody said anything. Almanzo's heart was pounding. A few boys in the back sniggered. *Probably Eddie and Elmer*, Almanzo thought.

"Five cents?" Miss Thayer offered, her smile fading a little.

This was too dreadful. Almanzo didn't have to know anything about girls to know that whoever had made that basket was probably dying of shame right now. Whether it was Catherine's or not, and as much as it scared him, he had to speak up.

"Twenty—" He stammered, cleared his throat, and had to start over. "Twenty-five cents," he said.

Miss Thayer gave him a look of deepest gratitude. "Thank you, dear. Sold for twenty-five cents to—"

"Thirty-five cents!" said a voice from the back of the room. Almanzo could not see who it was. Miss Thayer's face was a picture of surprise.

"Don't give up now!" Bert whispered in his ear.

"Um—fifty cents!" Almanzo said. He didn't want to drag this out too long. He hated everyone staring at him. Astonished murmurs were spreading around the room.

"Sixty cents!" said the strange voice.

"Seventy-five!" said Almanzo.

"What do you know that we don't?" Victor said, leaning over Almanzo's shoulder.

"Do you know whose it is?" Joshua asked. "Is she pretty?"

"One dollar!" said the voice at the back of the room.

"It must be someone good," Victor said. "A dollar ten!"

"A dollar twenty-five!" Almanzo said. He heard someone whisper, "Catherine Baldwin," and another, "Couldn't be Miss Baldwin's," and then, "Why else would they—"

Suddenly four more hands went up. "A dollar fifty!"

"A dollar sixty!"

"A dollar eighty!" the voices called out.

But now Almanzo was determined. He had started this. He was going to win that basket. If it *was* Catherine's, so much the better.

"Two fifty!" he cried.

"Two seventy-five!" said the mystery voice.

They climbed up to four dollars. Miss Thayer looked more and more surprised. Then Almanzo saw movement in the doorway. A few girls had dragged Catherine through the crowd. They pointed to the lonely basket and whispered in her ear.

Although they were not meant to notice this, Almanzo knew that all the boys in the room saw it happen. The bids paused for a long, tense moment.

Catherine looked at the basket. She looked at the bedraggled black ribbon. Her brow furrowed prettily. And then . . . she shook her head.

His heart sank. It was not her basket. Who was he bidding on? What if it wasn't even a girl from school—what if it was someone much older than him? But wouldn't it be mean of him to stop bidding now?

"So," Miss Thayer said faintly, shuffling her papers. "It was . . . four dollars, was it not?"

Nobody spoke. Whose four dollars were about to be thrown away on a mystery?

"I bid five dollars!" said the voice from the back of the room.

Some people gasped. Others turned, craning their heads to see who it was. Almanzo felt relief pour through him. He could not bid any more than that. The problem had been taken out of his hands. He felt exhausted, as if he had been wrung out like wet laundry. The auction was tiring enough; he could not imagine how he might have felt if he'd actually had to eat an entire picnic with a girl, whether Catherine or anyone else.

"Sold!" Miss Thayer said, banging her gavel. "The auction is over! You may all go next door to pay and collect your baskets. Thank you, gentlemen, we have raised a very impressive amount of money for our new library. I hope you all enjoy your picnics!"

There was a crush of people around the door, so it took Almanzo and Bert a few minutes to get through to the hall and then into the next room. The baskets were back on the desks, and girls were standing prettily beside them.

Almanzo felt an ache in his chest as he saw Catherine standing beside the pink, lacy basket. Her sweet, warm smile did not change when Eddie came up to her. She did not seem to mind his mean eyes and narrow chin. Perhaps she did not know what a bully he was. Eddie tucked his red hair behind his ears and flicked imaginary dust off his jacket. His chest was puffed up like a blue jay's. He talked even more loudly than usual, as if he knew that all the other boys in the room were watching him enviously.

There was no one standing beside the last bedraggled basket. Apart from Catherine's, it had sold for the most money. Everyone was curious about who had made it. But the girl who had made it was either hiding or hadn't been able to get through the crowd yet.

Alice thumped Bert on the shoulder in a very unladylike way when they came up to her.

"Ow!" Bert said. "But I got it right!"

"Oh, and you were very discreet about it, too!" Alice said. "You should have heard the other girls laughing!"

"Aw, they're just jealous," Bert said.

"Perhaps," Alice said, a little mollified.

"Jealous that you get to picnic with someone as dashing as *me*," he said.

"Albert Baldwin, I declare," Alice said, but she couldn't stop herself from laughing.

Almanzo moved away from them as they made plans for their picnic. He drifted closer to the unclaimed basket. And so he was within earshot when a woman finally walked up to it in a dazed, happy way. He could not believe his eyes. It was Miss Lowe, the music teacher!

"Five dollars, Miss Lowe!" said one of the girls from the class above his. "You should have heard them bidding! It was incredible!"

"Really?" Miss Lowe said, fingering the

black ribbon. "For my little basket?" Her face was glowing in a way he had not seen before. When she smiled like that, she almost looked pretty.

"The food inside looked really good," Almanzo said honestly. "Anyone would love a picnic like that."

Miss Lowe beamed at him.

But there was one more surprise. "Miss Lowe?" said the deep voice that had won the basket. Mr. Lloyd stood there, his mustache fluffing up as he smiled. He took her hand and bowed over it. "I am honored to be picnicking with you."

Miss Lowe seemed overcome with shyness. Almanzo knew he should not listen anymore. He pushed his way back through the crowd to Alice and Bert.

"I'll see you at home," Alice said to Almanzo.

Bert picked up the basket and pretended to stagger. "Gee, I wouldn't have bid if I'd known how heavy this was," he groaned.

"Oh, poor Albert," Alice teased. "Let's not

tell him that I carried it all the way here by myself, shall we, Manzo? We wouldn't want him to find out that a girl is so much stronger than he is. It's hard enough for him to know I'm smarter." She was out the door before Bert could think of a clever response.

They talked about the social later that night, at home. Almanzo told her how close he had come to winning Miss Lowe's basket. Alice laughed and laughed. But she thought it was sweet when she heard how thrilled Miss Lowe was about the bidding. She thought it was even more sweet when he told her that Mr. Lloyd was the one who'd won.

"So Miss Lowe isn't the girl for you," she said, laughing. "Don't worry, Manzo. You'll find the perfect girl one day."

What if I already have? Almanzo wondered, thinking of Catherine's happy smile. *And what if I already lost her?*

WILLY WILDER

On a warm summer day in late August, a young man stood on a train platform in Spring Valley, Minnesota. He was much taller than the boy who had left Malone a year and a half earlier. His face was brown from the sun, and his hands were large and strong. He was waiting for a train, but his gaze was on the horses tied up to the hitching post.

The Wilders were not leaving Spring Valley, not yet. They were still trying to figure out what to do about Aunt Martha and the two farms. Aunt Martha was thinking about selling her farm and moving in with her parents on the other side of town. If she did that, the Wilders could go back to Malone knowing she was in good hands. But they did not want to rush her into a decision, so they were waiting for her to make up her own mind.

Instead, Almanzo was at the train station because they were getting a visitor.

Almanzo lifted his head as the sound of the train whistle sang out. The puff of smoke on the horizon drew closer and closer, and then all at once the vast iron locomotive hurtled into the station with a shriek and a hiss and a cloud of steam. All around him, people pressed forward to greet new arrivals or to drag their luggage onto the train.

He remembered standing here the day they arrived. He remembered the confusion, and he remembered seeing Bert and Catherine across the platform.

He could imagine how his cousin William must feel, alone in a strange place after a long journey. But then, Willy was used to long journeys. He had come here all the way from India.

Two months ago, Father had received a letter from his younger brother, Royal, the missionary. After so many years in India, Royal was tired and ill. He wanted to come home for a rest and to meet with American doctors. He also wanted his children to start getting an American education. But they could not settle down anywhere until Royal was well. He was hoping to find relatives who would take in his children while he recovered. Would James and Angeline be willing to open their home to young William for a short time?

Father wrote back right away. Nothing would make them happier. Mother had started planning for Willy's arrival the day they got the letter. She was full of ideas for what to feed him and how to teach him about America and what Almanzo could show him around Spring Valley.

And now Willy was here. Almanzo would meet his long-lost cousin at last.

Everyone had been in such a flurry getting the house ready for a guest that Almanzo had been sent to collect Willy on his own. It made him feel very proud and grown up to drive the horses through town. He could not help hoping that Catherine might see him, even though he tried not to think about her. Alice reported that Catherine had been seen out walking with Eddie several times since the basket social. Perhaps if Almanzo had been braver before the basket social, that might have been him on her arm.

He stood up on his toes and examined the new arrivals. Which one of them was Willy?

Then he spotted a thin boy who looked close to his age. His skin was as brown as Almanzo's, although he was not so sturdy-looking. His clothes were clean and neat but threadbare. He wore oval steel spectacles perched on his nose. A small valise sat on the platform beside him.

"Willy?" Almanzo said, coming up to him. "Are you Willy Wilder, from India?"

The boy blinked owlish blue eyes at Almanzo.

"Hello, cousin. What a fascinating, strange place this is." He stared around at the perfectly ordinary train platform full of perfectly ordinary people as if he had never seen anything like it in his life.

"Where are the rest of your things?" Almanzo asked, feeling a little shy.

Willy waved his hand at the small valise. "This is all I have. We travel light in my family."

"All right," Almanzo said, taking the valise from him. "The buggy is right over here."

"The what?" Willy said, following Almanzo along the platform. As they came down the steps toward the hitching post, Willy stopped with wide eyes, staring at Queen and Thackeray. "What are *those*?" he breathed.

Almanzo was dumbfounded. "They're horses!" he said. "You must have seen horses before!"

"But where are the elephants?" Willy said. "How will we get anywhere without an elephant to ride?"

"We don't have elephants in Minnesota," Almanzo stammered. "But these are much better, these are horses—*horses*," he pronounced loudly and slowly.

"Oh," Willy sighed, clasping his hands together. "If only my monkey attendants were here to wait on me, I would feel so much better."

Almanzo goggled at him. A moment passed, and then Willy busted out laughing. He held his sides and laughed fit to burst.

"You should see your face!" Willy cried. "Like I just stepped off the moon!" Tears of mirth were streaming down his cheeks.

Almanzo started laughing too. "You're going to be trouble, aren't you?" he said, grinning. All his shyness was gone like a puff of smoke.

"Never seen a horse before," Willy chortled. "That *is* fun. I hope I can play this trick on a few more people before everyone catches on."

"Try it on my sister Alice," Almanzo offered. "She's very polite. She'll be terribly kind and understanding—it'll be very funny."

They climbed onto the buggy seat, both of them feeling as if they were fast friends already.

"Have you really ridden an elephant, though?" Almanzo asked as he turned the horses toward home.

"Of course," Willy said. "Hasn't everyone?"

"You're not going to fool me again," Almanzo said. "So how do you get on its back? Aren't elephants as tall as a house? And how big does the saddle have to be to go around its huge belly? And what do you hold onto, since there isn't a mane—its ears? Doesn't the trunk get in the way of the bridle? And *what* are you laughing at?"

"Sorry," Willy said, waving his hands. "Stop, stop, it's too wonderful. No, listen, there isn't a saddle—you ride in what's called a 'howdah.' It's like a box with two seats in it, and they strap it to the elephant's back with ropes. That's what we would sit in while the mahout steers—he's the elephant trainer, and he sits on the elephant's neck holding a long metal spear.

If he pokes the elephant behind its left ear, that turns it to the right; when he pokes behind its right ear, the elephant turns left."

"So there are no reins?" Almanzo asked.

Willy shook his head. "No. He steers with the stick and with his feet on the elephant's head."

This sounded very peculiar to Almanzo, but the more he thought about it, the more he reckoned it was not so different from horse riding after all. You could signal to a horse with your feet, too, although you did not use its ears to steer. But then, an elephant's ears were much bigger than a horse's. They had been riding elephants in India for hundreds of years, so they must have worked out the best way to do it.

All the way back to the farm, Willy told Almanzo more stories of India. He explained how the mahout would get the elephant to kneel by pressing on the top of its head. Then the riders could climb a ladder to get into the howdah. He also said that sometimes the elephants were painted in bright colors like pink and green and red and yellow, especially for the big Hindu festivals that seemed to happen every month.

"Mother wanted us to stay away from the festivals," Willy said, "but it's hard to ignore thousands of people standing in the river singing and worshipping. Especially the holy men who paint themselves yellow and have hair down to their feet."

"Are you serious?" Almanzo said.

"They're called 'fakirs,'" Willy said. "I wanted to talk to them, but Mother would never let me. I think that's really why we've all come back to America. She was afraid that my brother Eddie and I were becoming too native, talking in Hindustani and running around with nothing but our breeches on." He made such a comical face that Almanzo had to laugh, even though he was a little shocked.

"It was very hot," Willy explained.

"Hotter than this?" Almanzo asked. A thick, sweltering heat had been baking the town for the last week, and he almost looked forward to bath night just for the chance to cool off.

"Much, *much* hotter than this," Willy said. "In the dry season sometimes it was ninety-eight degrees all day *and* all night *inside* the house. We don't know what it was outside, because our thermometer only went up to a hundred twenty degrees, and it was something way above that. Father brought it inside because he thought it might burst. Mother let us sleep on the roof at night because it was cooler in the breeze up there, unless there were dust storms."

Willy talked about how they would get up very early in the morning so they could use as much of the day as possible before the noon heat set in. He said they always stayed indoors during the hottest hours in the middle of the day.

He told Almanzo about something called a "punka," an enormous fan that was hung from the ceiling in every room. The fan was made of muslin or light cloth attached to a frame. A rope went from the fan through the wall onto the porch outside. Every family had a servant whose job it was to stay on the porch all day, pulling the fan back and forth, back and forth, to make a breeze inside.

Sometimes they would also have door-size grass screens set in the wall. A boy would stand outside all day throwing water on the screen. Then when the wind blew through the screen, the water would evaporate and cool the house.

"All right, now you must be pulling my leg again," Almanzo said. "There's a man whose whole job is to pull the fan all day long? That's it?"

"That's India," Willy said with a shrug.

Almanzo could not wait to take Willy to school with him. He knew his friends would also be amazed by Willy's stories. If only Royal and Eliza Jane could hear them! Eliza Jane thought she knew everything, but Willy could tell them about things none of them had even heard of. And Royal would probably have all kinds of interesting questions. Almanzo hoped Willy would stay with them long enough to meet his brother and sister, and maybe even Starlight.

It was funny to think that two years ago Minnesota had seemed so far away. If Willy and his family could travel all the way from America to India and back, then there was nothing that could stop Almanzo from going even farther west from here, to the edge of the frontier where he could claim his own land and be a real pioneer. He had started dreaming big dreams about planting his own wheat and starting his own farm one day. It wouldn't be long before he was old enough to stake his own claim. Maybe Willy or Royal would come with him.

Still chattering, the boys pulled into the farmyard, where Mother and Father were waiting to welcome Willy with arms outstretched, and the warm smells of dinner curled out from the kitchen, inviting them inside.

TALES OF INDIA

Although Willy was only joking about never seeing a horse before, there were lots of things that seemed to confuse him. Almanzo was surprised to see that Willy was not used to the kind of food they ate. He almost never finished his bread. He said that in India they did not eat as much bread as they did in America. After a week, he asked if they could have rice for dinner one night instead of potatoes. He didn't know that rice was so much more expensive in America than in India. In

India he had eaten rice for dinner almost every night.

Willy told Almanzo that he missed something called "curry," which he described as a mix of chicken and hot spices that burned your throat when you ate it. Almanzo thought that didn't sound very good, but Willy said that everyone in India ate it and everyone liked it after a while. He said that food in America seemed very bland after curry. But he never said so to Almanzo's mother. He did not want to be impolite.

Willy drank tea four or five times a day, although he said that the tea in India was much more flavorful. He drank it with milk and sugar, in the English way. India was owned by the British. There were many more British people there than Americans. Sometimes Willy would imitate the funny way the British talked and make them all laugh. Sometimes he used words that they had never heard before, because he forgot that they did not speak Hindustani like he did.

When Father gave them a day off from farm chores, Almanzo took his cousin blackberry picking. He was sure this was something that Willy had never done in India. They brought little Perley with them. Now that he was walking and talking, Perley was even funnier than he had been as a baby. He loved to follow Almanzo around the same way Frank did, watching everything he did with big eyes.

Almanzo let Perley ride on his back as the boys climbed into the low green hills around the farm and searched through prickly thickets. Blackberry juice squished between their fingers and made their hands purple and sticky. They filled buckets to take back to Mother for blackberry preserves. The sun warmed them from head to toe, and they lay on their backs in the long grass, breathing the clean, wild air and watching the puffy white clouds chase one another around the blue sky. Almanzo gave Perley a small roll of nutty bread to chew on, and his little brother leaned contentedly against his knee, listening to the older boys talk.

"You were right," Willy said to Almanzo. "I like blackberries very much. I wish I could take you to India. I bet you would love the fruit there."

"Is it that different from the fruit here?" Almanzo asked. "We have apples all the time. And sometimes we get oranges, too. Back east there are plenty of blueberries and huckleberries. If we can find them there are plums and cranberries and strawberries. Isn't that enough?"

"You wouldn't think so if you'd ever tasted a banana," Willy said wistfully. "Or a coconut."

"Banananananana," Perley gurgled, hugging Almanzo's leg.

"What are those like?" Almanzo asked.

"Bananas are soft and pale yellow on the inside. You have to peel them like an orange before you can eat them. Coconuts are round and hairy, but when you crack them open, there is soft sweet white meat inside and a liquid they call milk, although it is sweeter than cow's milk. But my favorites are mangoes, which are golden and juicy and delicious. We ate them almost every day during the rainy season." Willy took off his spectacles and cleaned the lenses. "I should stop talking about this. It'll only make me hungrier, and I already miss the food we ate in India so much!"

Most of all he missed Indian sweets. He told Almanzo about a sweet shop at the Indian bazaar, which was a kind of market. Huge woven baskets overflowed with treats like molasses-sweetened doughnut balls and small, creamy squares made from milk and sugar. Willy's favorite were the bright orange *jalebies*, sugary deep-fried dough twisted into pretzel shapes. The sugar coating crunched as you bit into them and the warm syrupy taste was like eating sunshine and clouds.

But Willy cheered up when he discovered Mother's fluffy, light breakfast pancakes. He loved the sweet brown maple syrup. He ate a giant stack, soaking them in maple syrup first and covering each one in melting golden butter.

Mother was not sure that Willy was ready to go to school with his cousins. He had attended a school in India for the children of missionaries, but she was afraid it would not have prepared him well enough for the classes here. He told her that he was first in his class in Geography, Arithmetic, History, and Grammar, and second in Reading, Writing, and Spelling. Almanzo brought out the schoolbooks he used, and Willy had no trouble with the algebra problems or the advanced sentence parsing. Even Alice was impressed. Finally Mother agreed that Willy could go with Almanzo for the last month of school.

All the students thought that Willy was a great curiosity. At recess they gathered around him to ask questions. Even the girls came to join them. Almanzo was pleased to see that Catherine was one of them. She smiled her pretty smile when Willy told funny stories about monkeys and the villages he had seen traveling through India on his father's preaching tours.

Only Eddie and Elmer stayed away. Eddie snorted and said he didn't see what all the fuss was about. The brothers threw a ball back and forth on the other side of the schoolyard, pretending not to care that they had to play alone.

"Did you see alligators?" asked Bert.

"Yes," said Willy. "Although in India they are called 'crocodiles.' A man came to the house once with a baby crocodile he had caught in his fishing net. It was only four feet long." He held out his hands to show how long that was.

"*Only* four feet!" one of the little girls squealed. "That's how tall I am!"

"Didn't it bite you?" asked another.

"No, it couldn't," Willy said. "The fisherman had tied its mouth shut. But we could see its teeth sticking out!"

"Did you ride elephants everywhere you went?" Joshua asked.

Willy laughed. "No. Usually we rode in a small covered carriage pulled by horses. It looks like a stagecoach, but we call it a 'dak gari.' Sometimes if we had to get somewhere the horses couldn't go, like up the mountain, we would sit on palanquins. Those are covered seats with poles at each end, and men would carry us with the poles on their shoulders. And the British have built railroads to get between the major cities. They're not so different from the trains here."

Eddie swaggered over. Almanzo guessed he was bored with being left out. He looked cousin Willy up and down. He crossed his arms. Almanzo liked the way Willy looked straight back at him.

"India's nothing special," Eddie said. "I've been to Boston."

"Me, too," Willy said. "That's where the boat left for India."

"And I saw the circus in Chicago," Eddie said, his face turning red.

"I saw the canals in Venice on our way home from India," Willy said. "I took a train through the Alps and I saw the Crown Jewels in London."

"You're pretty scrawny," Eddie said with a

scowl. "Is that because there's no food in India?"

"I had scarlet fever last year," Willy said matter-of-factly.

"I bet you can't even lift a bale of hay," Eddie sneered.

"I bet you can't stand on your hands," Willy answered back.

"Well—I—that's not—" Eddie started to say, but the other pupils were already calling out, "We want to see! Show us!"

Willy hopped off the steps and handed Almanzo his cap. All at once he was upside down. His worn-down shoes were up in the air. He walked on his hands all the way around to the bench at the side of the schoolhouse. Everyone cheered when he flipped upright again. Almanzo could not stop grinning at the look on Eddie's face. Even Elmer was laughing at him.

So was Catherine. After school, he noticed that she left without Eddie. Perhaps it was not too late for Almanzo after all.

That night Alice came out to help him

in the barn. As they threw forkfuls of fresh-smelling hay down from the loft, he told her he thought Willy was very brave.

"Because he's been to India?" Alice said. "If our father had been a missionary, we'd have gone all that way, too. We wouldn't have had a choice."

"It's not only that," Almanzo said. "It's the way he stood up to Eddie. It seems like he's not afraid of anything. I can't even—" He stopped, embarrassed.

"Can't even what?" Alice said.

"Nothing," Almanzo mumbled.

"Can't even talk to the girl you like?" Alice guessed, her eyes twinkling.

"Well," Almanzo said, "I tried . . . once."

"You have to try harder," Alice said. "It's not fair, but girls have to wait for boys to be brave. Otherwise, how will she ever know you like her? If you don't do something, of course she will end up with the boy who's bold enough to ask if he can walk her home."

"Is that all I have to do?" Almanzo asked.

"Well, it's a start," Alice said. "She'll think you are quite the gentleman."

Almanzo pitched another pile of hay down, smiling.

"Although," Alice said, "I still think you can do better than Catherine, Manzo. I heard her asking Louisa how Indians like the Dakota and the Cherokee got here all the way from India. She doesn't even know they are two different kinds of Indians! And then she said, 'I mean, isn't India all the way in Africa?'"

Almanzo couldn't help laughing at Alice's imitation of Catherine's sweet, high-pitched voice and puzzled look. "Lots of people don't know geography," he pointed out.

"But don't you want a smart girl, Almanzo?" Alice asked.

Queen whinnied from below, as if she was agreeing with his sister. He shrugged. Whenever he thought about finding a wife, some far-off day when he was much older, he did think he wanted her to be smart and clever. But maybe Alice was wrong. Maybe

Catherine was smarter than Alice thought. Maybe she was the right girl for him, and he just had to be brave enough to do something about it.

WALKING CATHERINE HOME

The next day, Almanzo waited outside the schoolhouse. He waved good-bye to Alice and Willy as they set off for home. He rubbed his hands on his trousers. His palms were sweating. His jacket felt heavy on his shoulders. He was afraid that Catherine would laugh at him. He was afraid that someone else would see and make fun.

Before he could change his mind, suddenly she was coming out of the schoolhouse door.

"Bye, Amelia," she said brightly to her

companion, and hurried down the steps. She did not even look at Almanzo. She almost went right past him. But then Almanzo stepped forward and touched her elbow lightly.

Catherine jumped and looked around at him.

"Miss Baldwin," he said with a little bow. "May I see you home?" He was proud of himself for not stammering this time.

She colored prettily. "Oh," she said. "Why yes, you may." She took his elbow and looked around. "Where's your cousin? He could walk with us, too."

"Willy already left," Almanzo said, feeling a little dejected. But his spirits rose quickly as they strolled down the path to the town. Catherine's arm in his was warm and she laughed at almost everything he said, which wasn't much. Her coiled brown hair shone like polished wood in the sunlight, smooth and perfectly even. Her wide brown eyes sparkled. It was much less awkward than he had expected, because she did almost all the talking and didn't seem to mind how quiet he was.

The only trouble was how slowly she walked. Part of him wanted their walk to last forever. But the other part of him knew how much work there was to be done at home. They still had all the work of two farms to do. He could picture Father looking at his pocket watch and frowning. He knew Queen would be stamping in her stall, eager to be ridden. But Catherine took tiny steps in her little boots. She carefully avoided any mud in the road. She drifted along like a caterpillar crawling across the vegetable garden leaves.

"What a pretty day," she said with a sigh. "I do like it when the sky is so blue."

"Me too," Almanzo agreed.

"I saw a bolt of cloth in Hoxie's general store that is just that color blue," Catherine said. "I asked Mother if I could have it made into a dress. Wouldn't that be pretty? She said we would see, so I'm going to ask Father next. He always says yes. And then I must find some ribbons to match. You must tell me if you ever see any ribbons just that color."

Almanzo did not know what to say about dresses. "I like your ribbons," he said.

"Yes, but these are pink," Catherine said. "It would be very silly to wear these with a blue dress. Can you imagine? White ribbons would be all right, but they don't look the same against my hair. And of course I cannot wear brown ribbons. Or red! That would not look right at all."

Almanzo was not sure why. Alice had some red ribbons, and they looked perfectly nice in her brown hair. But he was afraid he might sound ignorant if he said this.

"One day I hope I shall have so many dresses that I can wear a different one every day of the week," Catherine said dreamily. "All of them will have lace and hoop skirts and come all the way from Paris. Did you know that Paris is the most fashionable place in the world? And I shall have gloves and shoes and jewels, too. I wonder what those Crown Jewels are like that your cousin saw."

"He said they were all sparkles," Almanzo said. "I imagine them like how the world looks in the sun after the first ice storm."

"Prettier than that, I'm sure!" Catherine said with a smile. "Imagine being a queen and wearing such jewels all the time! I think I would be a splendid queen. I'd wear a crown of diamonds on my head. Don't you think that would be pretty?" Almanzo reckoned that probably would be pretty. She tilted her face up and blew kisses to an imaginary crowd.

"I'd like to go west," Almanzo said. "That's my dream. There's so much land out there that nobody is using. I could plant miles and miles of corn and wheat and potatoes and anything else you can imagine."

"I like corn," Catherine said. "My favorite is hominy when it's warm and served with milk."

"Me too!" Almanzo said. He'd often watched Alice and Mother hull corn for hominy, peeling off the outer skin and cooking the dry yellow corn until it puffed into a warm delicious mouthful. He was pleased to find something he and Catherine both liked to talk about. He could say plenty about food. "Or with maple syrup. We had that for breakfast all the time in New York."

"And it is such a pretty color," Catherine said. "I once had a dress the same bright yellow color as corn, but Mother thought it made me look jaundiced. She said it was a color for little girls, so I haven't had a dress like that since. Oh, but perhaps I could have yellow ribbons! That is a good idea."

She squeezed his arm a little and he forgot to be dismayed that they were talking about ribbons again.

After he finally left her at the door of her father's store, tipping his hat politely, he walked until he was out of sight of her windows and then he ran all the way home. He reached the barn panting and gasping. Luckily Willy and Alice had started his chores for him. They teased him about Catherine until he had to go clean out the calf pens just to get away from them.

But they were not so pleased when the same thing happened the next day. Once again, Almanzo asked if he could see Catherine home, and once again she took his arm. She seemed to walk even slower this time. She chattered the whole way about the dress she was having made for the next social and how she hoped it would not be too cold to wear it and didn't it seem unusually cold to him and perhaps she could have a new wool dress for Christmas, maybe in dark green with gold stripes, wouldn't that be pretty?

When he ran up to the barn, Alice was standing at the door with her hands on her hips. "Father just came looking for you!" she said. "We told him you were fetching more water. You mustn't do this again, Almanzo. We could all get in trouble."

"What can I do?" Almanzo said. "I can't hurry Catherine. She wouldn't like that."

Alice shook her head. "Don't you think this farm is more important?" she asked. Almanzo thought that was a bit unfair. Bert had been walking her home from school almost every day since the basket social. Just because Alice could walk as fast as either of them did not mean Bert should get to have a sweetheart and Almanzo should not.

"But what if she's the girl I'm going to marry?" Almanzo said.

"Who's talking about marriage?" Father's voice suddenly said. He came around the corner of the barn, carrying an unlit lantern. He looked back and forth between them sternly. "Alice, I know that Baldwin boy has been courting you. But I hope you will think carefully before making such a serious decision."

"Me!" Alice protested. "Almanzo is the one you should be scolding."

"Both of you listen to me," Father said. "Don't be tempted to such a big step unless you are quite sure that you will be bettering yourself. Marriage is a life work, my children. It must not be taken lightly. Come, Almanzo, let's finish the chores."

As he cleaned out the stalls and milked the

cows, Almanzo thought and thought. How could he keep seeing Catherine and still be home in time to do all his chores?

Then he had a wonderful idea.

The next day when Catherine came out of the schoolhouse, she smiled sweetly at him as she always did. He said, "Miss Baldwin, with your permission, I have a surprise for you."

"Oooh!" she said. "I love surprises. Is it a new ribbon? Or candy? I love candy."

"It is even better than candy," he said proudly. He led her around to the side of the schoolhouse where the hitching post was. There stood Queen and their gentlest horse, Stella. Willy had ridden Stella to school that morning so she'd be there for Catherine to ride home. Queen tossed her head, and Almanzo thought how beautiful she looked in the afternoon sun. Her sides glowed red-brown-gold like the sunset over the autumn leaves in the New York mountains.

Catherine stopped. "What is this?" she said.

"I brought horses so we could ride home

instead of walking," Almanzo said. "This one is my own horse. I trained her myself. Her name is Queen." He stroked Queen's velvety soft nose, and the horse nudged his arm playfully, looking for carrots.

"I don't *want* to ride home," Catherine said. Her voice was not sweet and pretty anymore. "I want to walk!" She jumped away as Stella stretched her long, coal-black nose toward her.

"But why?" Almanzo said, puzzled. "I promise you Stella is a good horse."

"I don't care," Catherine said, taking another step back from the horses. "Horses are big, smelly, dirty brutes and I don't want anything to do with them. Really, Mr. Wilder! Did you spare even a thought for my pretty dress?" She smoothed down her rose-pink skirts. "I can't have it smelling like horse for the rest of the week! And the wind would quite wreck my hair. No, no, it won't do at all."

Almanzo felt as if he had opened a box he thought was full of candy and found rotten greens instead. Suddenly he could clearly see why Alice did not like Catherine. She was vain and spoiled. She thought only of her looks and her clothes. She was not very smart, and she did not care that she knew so little.

Worst of all, she did not like horses.

Catherine didn't even look very pretty anymore. Her face was screwed up in a sneer and her eyes were small and unfriendly. He couldn't bear the way she looked at Queen. Almanzo realized that he had made a mistake. How could he ever have liked Catherine?

She smoothed her hair and composed her features. "Well, I know you didn't mean to be so foolish," she said. "I will forgive you this time. You may still walk me home." Her dazzling smile came back, but this time Almanzo could see how false and empty it was.

"I'm sorry," he said slowly. "I can't do that. I couldn't leave the horses, and I must get home to do my chores."

Catherine looked astonished. "You don't want to walk me home?"

"My apologies, Miss Baldwin," he said, but

he didn't feel sorry. He was glad he had found out the truth about her before it was too late.

"Well!" Catherine said. "I never!" She turned and flounced away without looking back.

Almanzo took a deep breath. He leaned against Queen's strong, beautiful neck. "Don't worry, Queen," he said to his horse. "I will only marry someone who appreciates you as much as I do."

"Thank heavens," Alice said, coming out from behind the schoolhouse. "I hoped this would bring you to your senses." Willy and Bert followed her, grinning.

"You knew that would happen?" Almanzo said.

"Of course," Alice said. "Catherine complains about the smell of horses all the time. And the sound of horses. And the way they spatter mud when they trot down the street. And how big they are. Maybe you hadn't noticed, but she talks a lot."

Almanzo laughed. "I'm beginning to think

I wouldn't mind a girl who's quiet like me," he said.

He rode home with Willy while Bert walked with Alice. It would be autumn soon. The sky was streaked with white and gold clouds, and the wind smelled of cider and bonfires. Almanzo was glad that he did not have to think about Catherine anymore. It made his head feel lighter and clearer.

Someday he would go west, and out there he would find another girl—one who was smart and strong and determined and brave. She would love his horses, and she would be a friend and companion to him for the rest of his life. He would wait as long as it took until he found her.

HOMECOMING

Almanzo had stopped asking Father when they would be going home. He often wrote to Royal, asking about Starlight, and he still thought about his beautiful horse every day. But he was so busy, and he'd grown so used to Spring Valley, that he was starting to think they might stay forever. Besides, it was clear that Father didn't know the answer any better than Almanzo did. He hadn't expected to stay in Minnesota so long, but he, too, was busy. They were all happy there, even Mother, who had been worried about making new friends. Now she had so many friends that their house was always full of visitors, with dinners or meetings or sewing circles every few days— just the way Mother liked it.

So when changes happened all at once, it took Almanzo quite by surprise.

First, Aunt Martha announced that she was getting married to the man with the white horses. Almanzo realized that the proposal must have been what Martha was waiting for, and why she hadn't moved home with her parents. Now that she had a new husband, she could move to a new farm and start again. She was still young and hoped for a baby like Perley.

Martha seemed very pleased to be leaving behind her life with Uncle George. She told them she was grateful for their help, but ready to move on. It was odd to think they would not see her every day anymore, but Almanzo knew that Mother was the kind of person who would always stay friends with her.

Then Martha told the Wilders she would

sell them George's farm. That solved the problem of what to do with it, and it gave them twice as much land. Almanzo was glad that all their work on the other farm would end up being useful to them after all.

Soon after Martha got married, Father came riding in from town and told them that he had found someone to manage their land for a year. They could go back to Malone and sell the farm there. Finally, they could properly pack up the house and move—this time with Royal and Eliza Jane.

It was time to go home.

Then everything happened very quickly. After two long years in Spring Valley, it was strange to be leaving again. It was especially strange to be going back east. Every fiber of Almanzo's being wanted to keep going west, out to the open prairie. He couldn't wait to start his real pioneer life—to be done with school and starting his own farm! But for him there was one big reason to go home: Starlight. He didn't want to go west without his beautiful stallion.

. . .

"Manzo! Manzo, wake up! Look!"

Almanzo started awake. He had been dreaming of the Big Barn and their house back east. Pale dawn light sparkled off the frosty edges of the window, and for a moment he didn't know which home he was in. Then he remembered. It was the day they were leaving for Malone. Frank was curled on the floor below the bed. He looked up, startled too, and woofed once.

"Look!" Willy cried again. His face was pressed against the glass window pane. A red wool blanket from the bed was wrapped around his thin shoulders. His spectacles were crooked on his nose.

Almanzo rolled sleepily out of bed and came to the window, shivering in the early morning cold. Frank followed him and pawed at Almanzo's legs, demanding to be picked up. Almanzo lifted Frank and let the dog lick his ear as he looked out the window.

He could not see anything surprising. The farmyard was quiet and still. He could hear

Father starting the fire in the stove downstairs. A rooster strutted in one of the outdoor chicken pens, fluffing his feathers like he was thinking about crowing. Fat snowflakes drifted down from the thick gray clouds, piling up quickly on the cold ground. Already there was a thin dusting of white over everything in sight.

"What is it?" he asked. "I don't see anything."

"The *snow*," Willy said in a hushed voice. "Look how beautiful it is."

Almanzo squinted. The snow looked the same as any snow. It was the first snowfall of the year, but it was nothing special.

Then he realized something, and his mouth fell open.

"You've never seen snow before!" he guessed.

Willy shook his head, grinning. "I've read about it," he said. "And you could see it far away on the mountain peaks in the north of India. But I've never seen it falling from the sky."

"Well, you'll see plenty of snow this winter!" Almanzo said. Willy was coming to Malone with them. His older brother, Eddie, might join them there. It would be a full house for a while. Although there would be a lot of work to do, Almanzo was sure there would still be time for snowball fights and sleigh rides and roasting chestnuts and mulled cider around the blazing fire. There were many winter things that Willy had never done. Almanzo would make sure he didn't miss a single one.

Later that day, as they were packing the last trunk into the wagon, Bert Baldwin rode up on Velvet. He swung down and took off his cap to shake hands politely with Mother and Father. Alice looked like she was smiling and trying not to cry at the same time.

"I came to wish you all a safe journey," Bert said. "If there's anything I can do here to help, please write and let me know." He took Alice's hand and pressed it between his own. "I hope you come back very soon," he added. His words were for all of them, but his eyes were only for Alice.

"I hope so, too," Alice said with feeling.

"Thank you for your warm wishes," Mother said, and Father gruffly agreed.

"'Bye, Bert," Almanzo said, shaking his hand. "I know you'll take good care of Frank." Bert was going to take Almanzo's dog home with him until the Wilders returned. Frank's expression was confused as Bert slipped a lead rope around his neck, but he thumped his little tail on the ground agreeably.

"We'll be back in no time," Almanzo promised Bert and Frank. He couldn't wait to have everyone he cared about in one place at last—Royal and Bert, Frank and Starlight and Queen, Willy and Alice and Perley and Mother and Father. He felt he would even be pleased to see Eliza Jane again.

"Good luck!" Bert said. He winked at Almanzo and vaulted onto Velvet. With a tip of his cap, he trotted out of the yard, leading Frank behind him. The dog looked back a few times, surprised that Almanzo was not following.

Almanzo squeezed Alice's hand. He knew

how sad she was to leave Bert. He guessed she would miss him as much as he would miss Frank. He also knew that Bert would wait for her, no matter how long it took for them to return—and if it took too long, Bert would come out to Malone and find her!

The train journey back to New York went by in a blur. Almanzo remembered how amazed he had been the first time, and how big and loud everything had seemed to him. Now he felt responsible and grown up, carrying the luggage and holding their tickets and buying food for them all to eat in the different stations while Father made arrangements with the porters.

Royal was waiting for them when their train puffed and whistled into the station in Malone. He was leaning against the wall reading a newspaper. He was wearing a navy suit and a dark blue necktie knotted loosely under his collar. He looked taller and thinner and older, but he was still the same Royal with his long, serious face. The only difference was that now he had a thick, bristling brown mustache. He must have given up on the idea of a full beard.

"Why, Royal," Almanzo said as they shook hands, both of them grinning widely. "Don't you look fine! But I'm afraid you have something on your face."

"I do?" Royal said in surprise. He brushed at his chin and looked around for a looking glass.

"Yes," Almanzo said, leaning forward and nodding seriously like a doctor examining his patient. "It looks like a big hairy caterpillar has made its home under your nose." He shook his head. "I'm sorry, it's too late to save the rest of your face."

Royal swatted his head with the newspaper. "I see you didn't grow any manners along with your extra inches. You've sprouted like a weed!"

Almanzo grinned proudly. He might never be as tall as his long-legged brother, but Royal did not have to look down so far to meet his eyes now. He introduced Royal to Willy, and they went to help Father with the luggage as everyone climbed into the wagon. Royal pointed to new buildings in the town as they drove through. He told them all the latest news. He told them of a farmer who had come to see the house and might be a good buyer for the land.

Almanzo was only half listening. The pounding of his heart nearly drowned out Royal's words. Now that he was here, he could feel the excitement trembling through his whole body.

Perley leaned into Almanzo, chewing nervously on his thumb. He watched Royal with big eyes. Almanzo could tell that Perley didn't remember anything about Malone or his oldest brother.

"Wait till you meet my horse, Perley," Almanzo said. "Remember I told you about Starlight? Are you going to be brave when you meet him? You won't make any loud noises and scare him, right?"

Perley nodded, wide-eyed. He didn't take his thumb out of his mouth, but he whispered, "Bwave," around his fist.

"You'll have to be even braver than that

when you meet Eliza Jane, though," Almanzo said. "Then you might have to make loud noises—to scare her off, or she'll squeeze you and pinch your cheeks and straighten your collar and start teaching you about the thirty-seven states."

Alice laughed. "Manzo! Poor little Perley, don't listen to him."

But Perley knew that Almanzo was joking, and his worried look turned into a grin.

Almanzo pressed his hands together trying to keep still. He thought the drive from town had never seemed so long.

Finally, finally, they rolled into the old, familiar farmyard. Almanzo leaped out of the wagon before it had stopped moving and started running toward the Horse-Barn. He was already pulling open the doors before Eliza Jane even made it out onto the porch.

"Almanzo James Wilder!" she cried from the front steps, putting her hands crossly on her hips. "How can you want to see that *horse* more than your own sister?"

Apparently Eliza Jane had not changed very much, either.

"Go on, son," Father called. "But come back soon to put away these horses."

Almanzo ducked into the warm darkness of the barn with a smile on his face. Father understood. He knew what it was like to love a horse so much. Almanzo stepped across the wooden floorboards, his boots scuffing through the hay scattered across the floor. He breathed in deeply, filling his nose with the sharp sweet hay smell and the woolly sheep smell and the smell of horses that had been trotting in the wild winter wind, tossing their heads with their manes flying out behind them.

And then he was finally there. As if he knew Almanzo was coming, Starlight had his head over the stall door, watching his long-lost friend hurry toward him. Starlight's velvety ears pricked up, and his soft brown eyes seemed to shine with the same joy that Almanzo felt. He hadn't forgotten Almanzo at all. He pushed his nose into Almanzo's outstretched palm and nuzzled Almanzo's neck.

Almanzo ran his hand along Starlight's strong brown neck and under his fine black mane. The white star on the stallion's forehead glowed like a real star in the dim lamplight. Starlight was still the most handsome horse Almanzo had ever seen in his whole life, no matter how far he traveled.

"I'm back, Starlight," he said. "Are you ready for a great adventure? Father said Royal and I could bring you and the other horses to Minnesota by boat. You might not like that part, but oh, Starlight, you'll love the western prairies. The grass that goes for miles, the sky that never seems to end, the bright open air and the stillness when you're out far from everyone."

He leaned against the stall door and Starlight nickered quietly, flicking his ears.

"Just you wait, Starlight," Almanzo said. "We're going west—you and me together. Wait and see."

AUTHOR'S NOTE

Dear readers,
I've always loved Almanzo Wilder—
what Little House fan doesn't? We get to meet
him as a child in *Farmer Boy*, where he is funny
and real and so devoted to horses (and food!).
Then we have several books where we get to
know him better—courting Laura in *Little Town
on the Prairie* (my favorite!), driving her home
every weekend from the horrible Brewster
house in *These Happy Golden Years*, and, of
course, saving the whole town from starvation

in *The Long Winter* (my other favorite!). He's an honest-to-goodness hero and a genuinely good guy—and for me, he's always been one of the most believable, real characters in literature. Laura clearly loved him . . . so it's no wonder that we all do, too!

Of course, all of this made writing *Farmer Boy Goes West* a challenge in many ways. When I wrote *Nellie Oleson Meets Laura Ingalls*, I had much more freedom with Nellie's life, because there wasn't one *real* Nellie Oleson. That character was based on three different girls that Laura knew growing up, so when it came to writing her history, it was all right to use my imagination. Also, Nellie was the villain in Laura's books, so I didn't have to worry as much about getting her all wrong or ruining her character for readers.

But for Almanzo I wanted to stay close to his true history, while still telling a story worthy of the Little House series, not to mention worthy of a person who is so beloved.

There are some things we don't know

for certain about the Wilders' move. I found research that said Almanzo actually stayed home in Malone when they first went, but I also found information that said he went with them—and based on letters from Angeline to her other children, it sounds like he was in Spring Valley at least part of the time. We're not entirely sure why Almanzo's father, James, decided to move his family, when they were so prosperous in Malone, although it might have been because his oldest daughter, Laura Ann, had already moved out there, along with several other family members. And we don't know the exact dates of all their travels. So I had to imagine some of that as well.

The biggest change I made was speeding things up. Here's the actual history: The Wilders first traveled to Spring Valley in 1870 or 1871 and bought land adjoining Uncle George's. There's not a lot of information about what they were doing there all through 1872. Uncle George died in 1873, and then Aunt Martha quickly remarried and sold his land to the Wilders for $500. They were still there in 1874, and they didn't move the whole family out from Malone until 1875.

I wanted to tell the story of Almanzo's family deciding to move west and I really wanted to include his return to Malone and Starlight . . . but if we stuck to those dates, it would have been a very long book! And that seemed like such a long time for Almanzo to be away from Starlight, waiting to figure out what his family was going to do next. So I condensed their Spring Valley visit into two years instead.

In the Little House books, Laura changed several biographical details herself—including the ages of all the Wilder children. In real life, Royal was ten years older than Almanzo; Eliza Jane was seven years older; and Alice was three and a half years older. But in the second paragraph of *Farmer Boy*, Laura changed all that. She told us they were all closer together: Royal five years older than Almanzo, Eliza Jane four, and Alice a little more than a year older.

Not only that, but Laura left out their oldest

sister altogether. That's right—Almanzo had a sister older than Royal. Her name was also Laura, which might be why she isn't in the stories. It could have been pretty confusing trying to keep track of another Laura!

This means that when the family left for Spring Valley, the two they left behind to watch the farm were actually quite a bit older than eighteen and seventeen. But I decided to stick with Laura's version of the story—*Farmer Boy Goes West* is intended to be a sequel to *Farmer Boy*, so details like that needed to match.

And if Laura could do it, hopefully she won't mind that I did a little detail-fudging, too—especially when it came to Albert Baldwin. Bert was a real guy, and Alice really met him in Spring Valley and married him in 1878. They had two children, Myrtle and Leland. Alice and Almanzo were always close friends, and I thought it would be great to meet her future husband and have him be someone Almanzo really liked, too.

But when I did a little research, I learned

that Bert was nine years older than Almanzo. Which means he was only five years older than Alice in real life, but if I kept his true age in this story, he'd be way too old for them to meet him at school. That's one big thing I changed—I made him closer to Almanzo's age so that they could be friends. But I like to imagine that they would have been anyway. . . .

(I also found one source that said Albert went by Al, not Bert . . . but then I'd have had several scenes where the characters were Alice, Almanzo, and Al, and I thought that might get a little confusing! Sorry, Al . . . I hope you don't mind.)

The character of Catherine is entirely made up. Her purpose is to help Almanzo figure out what he likes in a girl (one who appreciates horses, for instance!). By the time we see him courting Laura in *Little Town on the Prairie* and *These Happy Golden Years*, he seems so brave and calm and capable, as if asking a girl out doesn't make him nervous at all. But I doubt many boys start out that way, and I thought it would be nice to see Almanzo learning to be the bold, courteous suitor he later became.

I also took some liberties with Aunt Martha's personality, since we don't know what she was really like. We think the Wilders probably stayed with her and Uncle George when they first arrived in Spring Valley, and I imagine that could have been stressful for everyone. I wanted to show Almanzo experiencing how unpleasant it is to live where you're not wanted, as a sort of foreshadowing of what happens to Laura later, when she has to live with the Brewsters. Almanzo's kindness in *These Happy Golden Years*, when he goes to rescue her every weekend, seemed like it could easily have come from a place of empathy and understanding, as if it had happened to him, too.

I tried to keep historical details as accurate as possible. Most of the places I refer to in Spring Valley were real—like J. C. Halbkat's store, Hoxie's, Parson's Stone Block, the Baptist church founded by Martha's father, and, most especially, the new two-story brick schoolhouse. "Jenny Lind" trunks were real, and Almanzo's parents could have seen the singer on her tour through America. Pullman sleeping cars on trains were just becoming popular around this time.

The card game "Authors" existed, and it sounded to me like something Alice would enjoy. Basket socials really happened (and boys really got in trouble for buying the wrong basket!). Richard Sears, whom we see briefly in the chapter titled "Noon at Last," really did cross paths with Almanzo when they both lived in Spring Valley; he grew up to found the Sears department stores that are still everywhere today.

There are a few quotes from the Wilders' letters that I tried to work in—for instance, Father's lecture about marriage in the chapter titled "Walking Catherine Home" is based on his actual words in a letter he wrote around this time.

Willy Wilder and his adventures in India were real, too. According to a letter from Almanzo's mother to Eliza Jane and Royal,

Willy came to stay with them in Spring Valley, and he would have been around Almanzo's age. I thought this would be thrilling to include—in an age of pioneers, imagine having a cousin who'd been all the way to India! Think of the stories he could tell!

Then I started to worry . . . what stories *would* he tell? What was life like for American missionaries in India in 1870? How could I find out?

Luckily, I found the perfect book to help me with this part of my research. It's called *Affectionately, Rachel: Letters from India, 1860–1884*, and it's a collection of letters written by the wife of a missionary as she traveled from Pennsylvania to India and spent many years there. It was exactly what I needed for the details of Willy's life, and it's a terrific read—Rachel was a very interesting writer, much like Laura, with a fascinating (though often sad) life story. The book is hard to find, but if you're at all interested in that part of history, it's worth reading!

Apart from Laura's own books, of course, there were a few other books and booklets that were immensely useful historical resources: *The Ingalls-Wilder Homesites* by Evelyn Thurman; *The Wilder Family Story* by Dorothy Belle Smith; *The Story of the Wilders* by William T. Anderson; and *A Wilder in the West*, the story of Eliza Jane in her own words, edited by William Anderson.

I especially want to thank Mary Jo Dathe for sending me her book, *Spring Valley: The Laura Ingalls Wilder Connection*, which is fascinating and was the most helpful resource I came across—I highly recommend it! There's so much more in it that I couldn't include, especially about the later years of the Wilders' life in Spring Valley, and the time Laura and Almanzo and their baby Rose spent there. This is one of the reasons I envisioned Almanzo's mother as such a kind, welcoming hostess—she always seemed to have relatives living with them and people around her to take care of.

For Little House fans today, there are terrific

museums dedicated to the Wilder family and their era of history in both Malone, New York, and Spring Valley, Minnesota (where you can see the church the Wilders helped to found). I was lucky enough to visit the Malone site and meet some of the amazing women who run the museum and give tours: so many thank-yous to Sandra Young, Dorothy Howe, Kathy Ellis, and Gail Lovejoy for being so welcoming and warm and generous! It was an incredible visit and a wonderful site, and I really recommend it to any Little House fan or history buff.

I hope Laura and Almanzo would approve of the changes I made to Almanzo's life story, and that they'd like seeing this book next to *Farmer Boy*. Most of all, I hope readers feel I stayed true to Almanzo's character, and that they still love him as much as they did in *Farmer Boy* and the other books. Hooray for Almanzo!

—Tui T. Sutherland (Heather Williams)